Death in Durrington

by Derek McMillan

Edited by Angela McMillan

2

First published by Createspace 2018

This edition 2019

All characters fictitious

The Ivy Mystery

"Who is that woman climbing the tree?" I asked Micah.

"Oh, you mean Ivy. Ivy Dore. I think she's after that cat of hers."

It was a tortoiseshell cat, we later found its name was Pushkin. As we watched she lured Ivy onto narrower and narrower branches before making a dash for the ground where the bemused cat stood and looked up at her as if slightly scandalised by her behaviour.

It was amusing up to a point. That was the point at which Ivy stopped struggling to get down, screamed something most unladylike and fell out of the tree, breaking her neck.

Micah is something of a first-aider. In fact, she is something of everything. She got to work to resuscitate Ivy while I got on the phone to the ambulance. Micah looked at me and shook her head. Pushkin came up to the body and tried to snuggle up to Ivy.

"It's too late for that," I thought.

"Look at this," Micah was pointing to a tiny hole in Ivy's trousers. Ivy didn't go climbing trees in a skirt.

"Moths?" I wondered.

Micah looked at me pityingly and revealed the wound beneath the hole.

"Airgun," she said, "This was no accident."

We looked around the area which was visible from the tree.

"One of us will have to climb it," said Micah.

"Won't the police think that a little odd?"

"Then do it before they get here. I'll keep watch."

I haven't climbed a tree since I was twelve. That is fifty-four years ago. I got as high as I could in the time but there were no convenient assassins with air rifles to be seen.

"We were watching Ivy. Her antics distracted us from the killer," Micah said.

The police and ambulance arrived at around the same time. We had to make statements at the station. They were less than pleased that Micah had tried to resuscitate Ivy. Apparently, it messed up the evidence.

"I'll leave her to die next time."

"She is dead, Mrs McLairy. There will be no 'next time'," was all the answer we got.

No sooner were we home than Micah was at work on her laptop hacking quite illegally into the police system. As she put it, 'It is as leaky as a colander anyway. Anyone could hack into it.' I don't know if the police took the same attitude but I kept my peace.

"They noticed the air gun wound and they are not treating it as an accident. They have extracted the airgun pellet and analysed the striations. This will be very useful if and when they find the weapon which fired it. Airguns of that muzzle velocity do not require a licence."

"How do you know the muzzle velocity?" I asked.

"Depth of the wound." She said impatiently.

"Wouldn't that depend on how far away the shooter was?" I asked.

Micah paused for a long moment and then said, "Yes." between gritted teeth.

"However, the police have not found any registration documents among their three main suspects at this time."

Pulling a notepad towards her, she wrote down in her neat handwriting:

"Bertie Dore

Shane Dore

Frank Raison"

"Bertie Dore is Ivy's nephew and heir. The police have been unable to get the information on how much he inherits because all her property is in the name of a Panamanian company. That David Cameron has a lot to answer for."

"Shane is Bertie's legal partner who also has a lot to gain.

"Frank Raison is her next-door neighbour with whom she had a running battle. He did use the immortal phrase 'I'll swing for you.' which is often thought of as a threat … or banter."

"Is there a husband?" I asked.

"No. He would be a suspect of course but he died some three years ago. He died falling out of a tree."

"Pardon?"

"Hm. Yes it was the same tree and one of the same causes. He was in pursuit of Pushkin who has apparently played this trick before. And no, I am not adding Pushkin to the list of suspects. She does not carry an airgun. Cats lack the opposable thumbs needed to operate one accurately."

"Some cats have them," I protested weakly.

"I had a good look at Pushkin and she was unarmed and we were watching her the whole time. You cannot have her as a suspect."

"Who do we talk to first?"

"Bertie and Shane. We can express our condolences."

Before we left the house, the telephone rang.

A familiar voice said, "Sekonda"

Sekonda runs a perfectly respectable escort business for people who like a bit of royal company. Although she does not resemble Princess Diana, her voice is spot on. She was born George Whyte but reinvented herself with the name of a watch. She also knew about everybody in Worthing and everything which was happening.

"You're investigating the death of Ivy Dore."

It wasn't a question.

"I have a piece of information for you. You will be grateful?"

"Yes."

"How grateful?"

"Twenty?"

"More like forty but you make up your own mind when I've told you. Ivy Dore's parents. You've heard the term 'rich but honest'?"

"Yes"

"It doesn't apply to them."

"That's all you have?"

"Believe me, Craig, it will be enough. When you have wound up the case, pay me."

Micah added the word, "Parents" to her list. After due consideration she added a question mark.

We had to knock on the door of Bertie and Shane for a while before there was any answer. This never augurs well.

In the end one of them (Shane, we later discovered) answered the door with a comprehensive "Uh?"

"We were very sorry to hear about the death of Mrs Dore," Micah ventured.

"Uh?"

Micah repeated herself.

"Uh? Oh I see. You mean 'Poison Ivy' That's what we used to call her. Huh, huh, huh."

"So you are not heartbroken by your loss."

Shane's eyes narrowed.

"Who the f*** are you, then?"

"Old friends," I lied. I am generally well-disposed towards people but I didn't actually know Ivy Dore until her unfortunate demise.

"Oh really," said Bertie, "she never mentioned a couple of old wrinklies to me."

"Craig McLairy," I said.

"Micah McLairy" said Micah.

"Can't place you," Bertie insisted. He looked puzzled.

"I've known Ivy since school,"Micah improvised. She is usually the most honest of people but she will sacrifice anything if we are on a case.

Bertie nodded.

Micah continued,"We were very sorry about Ivy's death. You know I witnessed it."

There was an exchange of looks between Bertie and Shane which did not go unnoticed.

"I did my best for her but there was nothing to be done. Poor Ivy died in my arms."

After that piece of flannel there was nothing for Bertie and Shane to do but to invite us in.

"Ivy wasn't the easiest person in the world to get on with," Bertie conceded.

"Oh. Why was that?" Micah asked innocently.

"Well. She did like to interfere. She just had to stick her nose in where it wasn't wanted. She couldn't accept that anybody else had a view on how to conduct their own life. Auntie always knew best," he added.

"Of course, we are very sorry that she is dead," Shane added hastily. Too hastily, we later concluded. It would normally go without saying that you were sad at the death of a relative, even an awkward one. If you need to tell people then you probably have reservations about your sorrow.

"This is a nice place you have here." Micah said. This harmless conversational gambit was greeted with an unexpectedly long silence. Eventually, Shane, who seemed to wear anger like a shirt, blurted out.

"Well, of course, Auntie paid for it. And, of course, she thought that gave her the right to boss us around. I mean to say I am over eighteen and it really is, I mean it really was, none of her business if we went out clubbing or what time we got home or whether the kitchen was tidy."

I will say now that I have seen and smelt a worse kitchen once but only in a house rented by five very slovenly students. And when he said "I am over eighteen," it somehow made him seem very young.

"and der der der der." Shane gave a gesture which indicated the impossible demands of his interfering aunt.

Bertie started to laugh at this but then thought better of it.

"So tell me, what do you do?" Shane asked. He wanted to change the subject.

"I freelance for the Worthing News," said Micah.

This was perfectly true. They never published anything she wrote for them except a piece about fly tipping which they never paid her for but she did freelance for them.

"How about you?"

"Well, I'm between jobs at the moment. We both are."

….

"Lousy ungrateful layabouts," Micah observed at our business meeting in the bar of the John Selden.

"Lousy ungrateful murdering layabouts?" I queried.

"The police found no evidence. They both alibi each other which is useless in law because they are partners. An extensive search did not show up an air gun of any type but they would have disposed of it. A search of the area of the killing didn't lead to any useful finds either. We could put a question mark in brackets next to the murdering part. There is plenty of evidence for the rest of my description though."

She matched the deed to the word and wrote that in her notebook.

"This afternoon we offer our condolences to the parents Sekonda warned us about."

"That sounds like a plan. Do you fancy the fish for lunch?"

The John Selden served up something the size of Moby Dick and even the pair of us struggled to do justice to it.

Our next visit was to Ivy Dore's parents.

"Mr Sheldon?"

"Call me Clive."

Micah went through her routine of condolence and the pair asked us indoors for a very passable dry sherry.

"Ivy, ah Ivy, she was a tree-climber even as a wee lassie," Mr Sheldon was about as Scottish as Durrington but he seemed to be using it as a term of affection. He went on to talk at length about Ivy's youthful tree-climbing activities.

He made a remark which I found ambiguous. "Many a time and oft I had cause to warn our wee Ivy." Against what? Climbing trees or getting murdered?

"Did you notice the wife?" Micah asked as we strolled home.

"What about her?"

"She said nothing but her facial expression spoke volumes. She was nervous the whole time 'Call me Clive' was chuntering on. It was almost as if she were worried that he might tell us something about Ivy that would give the game away. The problem is that we don't know what the game is as yet. I think Sekonda was right to put us on to them though. The police have only questioned them in a perfunctory fashion so far. We need to find out more."

"Finding out more" for Micah meant exercising her dark arts on the computer. I reflected that nobody's bank account, facebook, twitter, online purchasing record, web history or criminal record was safe from my darling wife. What a criminal she could have made, were she so inclined.

I left her to it and went off to talk to Ivy's antagonistic neighbour, Frank Raison. En route I decided the most useful nosey parker I could imitate was a reporter. I had a press card of course and unless you have seen a real press card it looked quite authentic enough. Interestingly I have never had to produce it. People just assume that if I come from the Worthing News then I am telling the truth. That is strange behaviour for a reporter you might think. I couldn't possibly comment.

"That witch?" was his unpromising opening.

"That recently deceased witch you probably want to express your condolences for? If it is all the same to you I might just drop the word 'witch' because my readers don't like it, not when applied to the dearly departed."

He had the good grace to smile and invite me in for a cup of tea or 'something stronger'. I thought a wee dram might loosen his tongue but it turned out to be a very wee dram and the whisky was spelt 'whiskey.' Those who spell so badly seldom produce good drinks.

It seemed that Frank's tongue did not need loosening on the topic of "that witch" though. Once he got started he took me through the key issues. These included her washing line being an embarrassment, her 'bloody cat' dirtying his garden, her 'disgraceful' lawn and her irritating voice.

None of these sounded like a motive for murder in and of itself. I also knew from Micah's researches that the police had not found an airgun in the house or in the shed. They had also dug up his garden. He gave me a good fifteen minutes on that topic.

The lack of the murder weapon was hardly conclusive. The number of murderers who inconsiderately dispose of the gun, knife, candlestick or other blunt instrument is depressingly large.

I went home to report all this to Micah. She was obviously quite pleased with her researches and paid scant attention to my lack of useful information.

"It is all to do with the Panamanian company. You know, the one Ivy had her money tied up in. Ivy was not a financial operator and many of the business negotiations were carried out by none other than 'Call me Clive' through a shell company."

"A company that sells..."

"Shut up and listen, Craig. You know very well that a shell company is one which is used solely for financial shenanigans. In the case of 'Call me Clive' he had eight shell companies nesting inside each other like one of those Russian dolls. That is as many as I know about so far. It has been fascinating.

"They are not all registered in Panama, though most of them are. When the layabouts come to get their hands on the spondulix they will find that it has been syphoned off into another shell company if that isn't a mixed metaphor. That company cannot be traced back to 'Call me Clive" but I would bet my pension that either Clive or his silent partner, Grace, will benefit in some way from the wee girlie's money."

I poured her a drink. I poured myself one too, anything to take away the taste of that awful 'whiskey' Frank was slowly killing himself with.

We sat by the fire to consider the facts.

"So, Mr Sheldon had been robbing Ivy on the pretext of looking after her tax affairs."

"Yes," said Micah, "he charged his own daughter a considerable fee to keep her money out of the reach of the tax man. Then as soon as she was dead the whole sum was transferred to this anonymous shell company. That just leaves the small matter of proving he is a murderer."

"I've got an idea."

That statement was undermined by the look of incredulity on Micah's face. Mock incredulity, I hope.

I made a phone call, occasionally I asked Micah for help with some of the details. When I had finished, she looked at me with incredulity again.

"You can't do that!"

"Because?"

"It's unethical."

"Not as unethical as robbing your own daughter and murdering her."

"No," she conceded after a long silence.

That evening we had a visitor.

"Come in. Can we offer you a drink?"

Bertie sat down with an improbably large vodka. He put his phone down on the table and, after a couple of false starts, it started to replay his recording of a conversation with Clive Sheldon.

"What can you tell me about this, Mr Sheldon?"

"What is all this? Half a million pounds were transferred from one company to another. What has this got to do with me, I'd like to know?"

"I am Ivy's heir. Her estate consists of her property in the UK but there is exactly no money. That cannot be the case, can it?"

"I don't see what you are moaning about. You're not Ivy's nephew, you're her husband's nephew. You have no right to a single penny."

"Why did you have control of Ivy's money?"

"None of your business but let me say this. Who would you have controlling her money? A shiftless ignorant little squirt like you?"

"You were in charge of her money and now there isn't any."

"You didn't have the brains to look after it, that's all."

"You had the brains to steal the money and the airgun to kill her."

"You will never prove anything, you little oik. Yes I killed her. Yes I took the money. You will never prove a thing."

"Bingo!" was Micah's overenthusiastic response.

"I thought it was only in 'Murder She Wrote' that villains confessed," Bertie objected.

"To be honest, Bertie, so did I," I said, "Now can you get this phone down to the cops?"

Bertie gave me a look which was equally made of resentment of my distrust and contempt for anyone over the age of twenty.

Eventually, he said, "Yes."

The case of the missing candle

Micah and I were enjoying a bottle of Beaujolais Nouveau in the John Selden after a hard day's complete lack of work. Things were a bit slack for the Durrington Detective Agency just then. Suddenly the calm was broken when Micah's mobile made a noise. Barker was immediately alert and up on his feet growling at the phone as if it were an imprudent rabbit he fancied for dinner.

"Yes… yes…. Oh, I see….yes..."

Micah's end of the conversation was not very enlightening. She was scribbling notes in the old notebook she took with her everywhere and when she looked up at me she was beaming in a way which suggested we had a paying client.

"It's Father Cedric. It seems somebody has stolen the Easter candle from the church."

I nodded. It didn't seem like a cause celebre.

"And then they returned it."

I looked puzzled. So did Barker.

"Father Cedric would not have noticed but he happened to leave his keys in the sacristy and went into the church at 3 pm to collect them. The candle was missing then. He searched the church quite thoroughly but it was nowhere to be seen. By the time he went back to the church for mass at 6 pm the candle had been returned."

"Had there been a break-in?" I wondered.

"The church was open for adoration in the Chapel of the Blessed Sacrament from lunchtime onwards so nobody needed to break in. And provided they made no noise they could have been in and out without anyone in the Chapel being any the wiser."

Micah tapped her notebook.

"I have the adoration rota here."

The first witness we spoke to was Queenie Beaufort. She was on the rota from 2 to 3 pm. It turned out that the burglar could have made as much noise as a herd of elephants for all she was concerned. Her hearing aid was due for some replacement batteries but the shop wouldn't have them in for a week. It made the interview quite difficult but fortunately, she was a very good lip-reader.

None of the other people on the rota had noticed anything and by now it was getting late so we called it a day. We arranged that we would interview Father Cedric after morning Mass. We don't go to morning Mass nearly enough and I wondered fleetingly if this was old Father Cedric's cunning plan to get a couple of strays back into the flock.

The next morning, *More Radio* had news of a much more interesting case. It seemed that a man who rejoiced in the name of Adrian Portentous had been killed - "stabbed and mutilated" the report said. This was in one of the many twittens or narrow pathways with which Durrington is well endowed and it took place yesterday afternoon or "in broad daylight" as the report had it. A man was helping the police with their inquiries.

I wanted more details and Micah was already using her dark arts to access the police computer network.

"The victim was killed with a small knife which was the same implement used to castrate him, what the radio coyly referred to as a 'mutilation'. The man who is helping the police with their inquiries is the identical twin brother Andrew Portentous, who also lives in Durrington. There had been a previous altercation when Andrew found Adrian having sex with his wife, Cynthia. He had apparently driven him from the house vowing to cut his testicles off. The threat was overheard by the neighbours," she said.

"Andrew did not blame his wife because 'who could resist such a devilish handsome fellow' as his identical twin. He does sound a tad deranged."

"For the police, the evidence remains circumstantial until they can find the murder weapon. It may contain DNA from the victim or even a fingerprint from the murderer."

"The DNA would be useless. Identical twins have the same DNA."

"I would like to see a tricky defence lawyer arguing that Adrian had stabbed himself and then cut his crown jewels adrift while dead. The forensic evidence points to that sequence of events," was Micah's considered opinion on that.

"Any bloodstained clothing?"

"Andrew had just finished burning a lot of old clothes in an incinerator when the police arrived. The neighbours weren't happy about that either."

"Anyway," she looked at her watch, "it is time for Mass."

There was a surprise at Mass. Inspector Tillotson could not be described as a regular churchgoer. In fact he had made some childish disparaging remarks about transubstantiation and tended to amuse his colleagues with jokes about "throwing another papist on the bonfire". The surprise was that he was sitting at the back of the service keeping an eye on things.

After the service, Micah engaged Father Cedric in conversation in the sacristy while I remained in silent contemplation in the main body of the church. Tillotson remained in quiet contemplation of me.

The only knife I carry is a non-violent smoker's knife from my pipe-smoking days. It has a blunt blade suitable for raking our the pipe bowl and a spike for cleaning the stem. It was the latter that I used.

While Tillotson looked on I thrust the spike into the Easter candle. It was a substantial candle as it was expected to burn for a year on and off. On my third thrust, I struck metal. I turned to Tillotson.

"I think you've got chummy bang to rights, Inspector. Unless I am mistaken Portentous thrust his small knife into this large candle after he had finished trimming his brother.

"It must have been a crime of passion," Tillotson replied.

My surmise was correct and Portentous wound up with a substantial sentence for murder and mutilation. This was even after the judge had heard evidence that he was not of sound mind after his brother's hanky panky with his wife.

The local papers were full of the story of the police taking an Easter Candle into custody.

I wrote to the *Worthing Herald* to say that the candle was not in custody, it was merely helping the police with their inquiries.

03 Death by Computer

Inspector Tillotson was a good policeman, as he would be the first to tell you. And with the exception of Jews, Muslims, lefties and, of course, Catholics he was your ideal equal opportunities copper.

Imagine my surprise when he turned up in the John Selden and came to sit at my table. Me! A leftie and a Catholic to boot.

My surprise shaded into astonishment when Ben Tillotson bought me a drink. He even gave some biscuits to Barker. Barker does not care who he gets biscuits from.

Old Ben eyed my Cabernet Sauvignon with the sort of look he reserved for homosexuals and racial minorities. He opted for a pint of Harveys, an excellent choice in my view.

He noticed me looking at the door.

"Waiting for someone, Colin?"

"Craig."

"Whatever."

"I am expecting Micah any minute," I said.

"You can go on expecting. She has been arrested," With a look of satisfaction, he took a swig of his pint which clearly met with his approval.

"Arrested?" I said like an idiot.

"You heard me, Charlie, We've got Micah 'bang to rights' as you would say, though no policeman has used that phrase since Dixon of Dock Green. By the way, do you happen to know the password to her laptop?"

I ventured to suggest that nobody knew the password but had they tried asking her?

"Oh yes, we did that. She gave the password to our IT boffin straight away and as soon as he used it the computer froze. By the time it unfroze it had performed a low-level format on the hard drive and overwritten it with a mass of random data. A masterly job, the IT boffin said, but it was all in vain."

"Oh really?"

"Yes really, Charlie. We know all about the mirror in Switzerland."

"The what in where?"

Tillotson sighed, "You know a lot of people of your age go to Switzerland for assisted suicide, don't you? Well both you and Micah are going out with me and a rather prepossessing young WPC in," he looked at his watch, "half an hour from now. I trust the assisted suicide won't be necessary because I know you are going to be sensible about this."

Tillotson made a great show of putting the handcuffs on me and escorting me from the John Selden. This amused the clientele no end. They raised an ironic cheer when the Inspector had to bring me back in to pay the bill. Then it was off to Gatwick Airport tout suite.

I met Micah who was handcuffed to WPC Dolly Manger. She may or may not have been prepossessing. I only had eyes for Micah.

We embraced awkwardly because of the handcuffs.

"Look, are these really necessary?"

"What, with a pair of desperados like you? Of course, they are."

Then Micah demonstrated one of the tricks she was full of and slipped out of the handcuff. She rubbed her wrist and said "Ooh that's better," and smiled. Tillotson signalled the WPC not to engage in the fruitless activity of putting the cuffs back on again.

We had endless trouble with the metal detector at the airport but Tillotson waved his warrant card about and the officials eventually let us all through and we boarded the Swiss Air flight to Geneva.

There were similar problems at Geneva and Tillotson was beginning to rue the whole handcuff episode as being more trouble than it was worth.

We went to a grey anonymous building and the four of us attempted to squeeze ourselves into a small booth with a thin terminal connected to an impressively massive mainframe which housed a thousand mirrors of sensitive computers around the world.

"Two things I want to make clear," old Ben said, "One is that there is to be no funny business or you might have to take up that assisted suicide option for yourself and Mr McLairy. You didn't hear that, WPC Manger."

"And the second thing is this. I know your computer has been used to hack into private networks including the police national computer. We are not concerned with that here. Our sole concern is the use of this computer to kill Franco Bartelli by hacking into the operating system of his pacemaker and taking his heart places it wasn't supposed to go."

It was not the first time I had heard of Franco Bartelli and I looked a question at Micah. She, in turn, looked a "shut up and look innocent" at me and I maintained a discreet silence.

In the silence, I thought about the Bartelli case. We had been tipped off by a low-level employee that Bartelli, of Bartelli and Bartelli Investment Brokers, was up to no good with the futures market. The complex scam involved moving large amounts of other people's money about with a fair amount of it being moved into the Bartelli pocket. The Serious Fraud Office were not about to pay us for any information received. However, two national newspapers had offered us a lot of money for the exclusive rights to the story. Newspapers are unreliable clients so we made sure we had a contract with the one we eventually chose and cash in advance for investigations.

And with Bartelli dead all this lovely money was forever beyond our reach. Wherever he'd gone it was unlikely he was up to anything illegal.

"Ben, if and when I unlock this mirror, what on earth are you going to do with the information?" was Micah's question.

"The data will be transferred to another mirror more conveniently placed in the UK where we can examine it in depth. Remember we are only interested in the death of Bartelli, not anything else we might find on this computer," Ben Tillotson replied.

It was either accept this assurance or explore the assisted suicide option. We decided to accept the assurance. Micah gave the password. It was only one digit different from the code which would erase all of the data so it was rather important that Inspector Tillotson got it right.

Within half an hour all the data had been transferred. Micah changed the password which seemed akin to bolting the stable door after the horse has gone elsewhere but I didn't say anything.

"What happens now?"

"You will be remanded in custody while we plant the evidence," smiled Ben. "Only kidding. At least I'd like you to think that."

"Do you have any interest in finding out who actually killed Bartelli now you already have 'a body' for the crime?"

"I thought you'd never ask," was the unexpected reply.

"I know a little place we can go for a meal and I will lay out the information for you there. The staff are very discreet... or Swiss as we put it."

Micah had her notebook on the table and was taking copious notes while Tillotson engaged in a surprising feat of memory. He obviously had the files in his head.

"We are looking for someone with high-level computer skills," he began.

Micah made a noise like a snorting horse.

"You had something to say, Micah?" he asked politely.

"Only that the high-level skills would consist of typing "how to kill someone with a pacemaker using a computer" into Google. It is surprising what you can find out there."

She smiled sweetly and Tillotson continued.

"We were looking for someone with high-level computer skills but I have had a response from our IT crowd and they say that, although there are many strange things on the laptop there is no evidence of tampering with Mr Bartelli's pacemaker."

He had the good grace to remove my handcuffs at this point. I was pleased because they were interfering with my enjoyment of the lasagne.

"Just one thing," added Tillotson, "why are there a thousand thumbnails of garden sheds on your computer?"

"It's just a hobby," Micah responded.

Tillotson was all business again, "There are three other suspects. They have low-level computer skills as far as we know but as you say they can probably Google with the best of them."

Micah looked expectant with her pen poised over her notebook.

"The brother, George Bartelli, stood to take over the financial consultancy side of the business if Franco kicked the bucket and, indeed, he has now done so. He is a nasty piece of work but that is not a criminal offence, more's the pity."

"The wife, Thelma Bartelli, thought she stood to inherit a great deal of money when Franco shuffled off this mortal coil. She was wrong. The money all went to the third player in this unholy trinity.

"Suzi Wright is an artist's model. Franco must have been quite an artist in his own way because his bank details show that he paid her £150 a time for modelling sessions in her flat on Broadwater Road. They usually lasted an hour and..."

"We get the picture," Micah interrupted. "And, Ben, come on. You never suspected me of killing this low-life, did you? It was all a ruse to get the Durrington Detective Agency to help with your inquiries."

"Don't be like that, Micah. You know you can use methods which are forbidden to the regular police and like any upright citizen..."

"or desperado," Micah interrupted.

"Like anybody, you would like to help the police and see the villains put behind bars, wouldn't you?"

"Yes," Micah sighed.

Before we finished lunch, Micah had provided old Ben with a list of components which would be required to interfere with the workings of an Implantable Cardioverter Defibrillator and thus kill someone with a pacemaker remotely. The cost was less than £200.

"It is not likely they will have used their credit card to make the purchase but never underestimate the stupidity of the criminal fraternity. I will also need to know exactly which kind of ICD our Franco had and what was the evidence that he did not die of natural causes."

"Well," old Ben mused, "the second part is simple. He was as fit as a flea one minute and dead as a doornail the next. Pardon the cliches."

"A heart attack will do that for you," Micah said mildly.

On the way back to England she was muttering to me. She needn't have bothered because old Ben was obviously quite taken with Dolly Manger and paid more attention to her than his erstwhile prisoners.

The flight was uneventful. The turbulence was considerable as we were crossing the channel and it helped to concentrate on what Micah was saying. It took my mind off the 40,000 feet of empty and turbulent air below us.

"The only proof will be if the miscreants have left any evidence on their computers or any of the devices which they would need, radio aerials for example. If they have brains they will have erased any trace from their computers or used someone else's computer. That is what I would have done. I assume if the boys in blue have the nous they will have their hands on the laptops and when old Ben gives me mine back I will find out what information the police have been able to obtain. Their IT people seem quite efficient."

They were not efficient enough to stop Micah using her dark arts to hack into their systems and find out what they knew.

"They have George's work computer, his laptop and his phone. Thelma claimed not to know anything about computers at all but a search found a state-of-the-art laptop under her bed. Online contact was a big part of Suzi's business model and she had three very expensive laptops in her flat. She raised Cain about the police stopping her from carrying on her business."

"And the results?"

"Zilch, nada, nothing, in that order. Either they didn't do it or they covered their tracks as I thought they would. Alternately the murderer used a different computer – one they had no links with – to carry out the crime."

Micah looked thoughtful as I left her to take Barker for his evening walk.

She still looked thoughtful when I returned. "I need to check something out at the local library but it is possible that some person might use a library computer to access a spoof IP address to send an anonymised message. The whole business ought to be untraceable because the local library would allow a laptop to be used on its wi-fi."

"And in English, that means?"

"Oh come off it, Craig. You aren't a complete luddite."

"Humour me."

"It means they could have used the local library to make their communication anonymous whether they used a laptop or the desktop in the library."

"If it is untraceable to the police then it would be untraceable to us, wouldn't it?"

Micah subsided and asked about tea.

Over the tuna pasta bake, I casually mentioned, "I will be going to see Suzi Wright tomorrow."

"Unless you are going to brush up on your artistic technique, Craig, **we** are going to see Suzi Wright tomorrow."

"She isn't expecting you."

"Then I will be a nice surprise for her, won't I."

Suzi Wright was, it seemed, not used to her gentleman callers having their wives along for the ride but she took it in her stride.

"I want to ask you a few questions," I began.

"My fees are £150 an hour," she looked at us each in turn, "I am tempted to raise that to £300 under the circumstances."

"Thank you, Ms Wright, but our only concern is to help Inspector Tillotson eliminate you from his inquiries into the death of Mr Bartelli. If you would prefer it if we didn't then we quite understand," I said.

We got up to leave.

She gestured for us to sit back down again.

"OK, I will answer your questions free of charge. Just get a move on will you, I have a paying client coming soon."

"How much did Mr Bartelli leave you in his will?"

"None of your damned...oh well it was about 200 thousand pounds but it has to clear probate, whatever that is, so I haven't seen a penny of it. I only hope those bloodsucking lawyers don't keep too much of it."

"Were you aware that Mr Bartelli had a heart condition?"

"Well if so I blame that bitch wife of his. He certainly didn't act like a man with a heart condition if you see what I mean," she gave a smile which reminded me somehow of a shark.

"Mr Bartelli died at about 3 pm on the 3rd of January. Where were you at that time?"

"I can't rightly remember. Was it a Tuesday?"

"A Wednesday."

"Then I was here," She consulted a book and continued, "I was entertaining a Mr Smith. They give such original names. I know he was a police officer because he brought his own handcuffs, if that helps, but I have no more details than that."

"Are you planning any trips away from Worthing in the near future."

"None."

"Not even with your 200 thousand?"

"That will go straight into the building society for my retirement fund. I can't keep this lark up forever," and she treated us to the sharky smile again.

We made an excuse and left.

"THAT DIRTY RAT!"

Thelma's response to our condolences was not the text-book example of grieving widow. She was grieving for her expected inheritance rather than her cheating husband.

"And how come he has the energy to get up to no good with that whore when he didn't have any time or energy for his lawfully wedded wife?"

We didn't actually have an answer which Thelma would have liked to that question but Micah made sympathetic noises and eventually Thelma settled down enough to answer questions.

She knew nothing about the provisions of Franco's will. That cut both ways. She might have been outraged by the will and killed him or blissfully unaware of the will and therefore had a mercenary motive. Or, of course, Franco just died of natural causes. Micah insisted on this alternative solution for some time to come.

She had no alibi for the time of the death but there is nothing so suspicious as a water-tight alibi. Her relationship with her husband was, after she had run through her extensive repertoire of abuse, "cooling." Perhaps Arctic might have been more accurate.

George Bartelli made all the right noises about his brother's sad demise. He would be sadly missed as a business colleague but most importantly as a brother. In the end, Micah had to lend him a hankie.

George Bartelli had a cast-iron alibi. He was involved in a three-way video conference with two other business associates in Milan and Paris. It would be easy to verify.

Micah cross-checked the information we had with the information on the police computer. We were beginning to think Inspector Tillotson was deliberately leaving channels open for us but we were not complaining. Everything the police had squared with the information we had. No evidence of wrong-doing, no purchases of unusual technological equipment and no reason to think Franco hadn't died of natural causes.

Then we had a stroke of luck.

"Hello, Durrington Detective Agency?"

"Yes. How may we help you?"

"I think it is the other way round. I can definitely help you."

"Who's speaking?" I asked although I had a suspicion as to the caller's identity.

"You don't know me."

"Yes, I do. You're Caroline Pickett."

There was a pause.

"You have a distinctive voice, Miss Pickett. Can you meet us at the John Selden in, let us say, half an hour so we can talk face to face?"

She agreed with some reluctance. She clearly wanted to be anonymous for some reason and I had put the kibosh on that.

Micah resorted to her dark arts on the laptop to search the records of Bartelli and Bartelli. Caroline Pickett had been sacked shortly after the death of Franco. She had been the one who had told us about his dodgy dealings on the futures market and received an appropriate fee for the information. It was hardly surprising that I had recognised her voice.

"I understand you've lost your job at Bartelli and Bartelli. Surely they can't just sack people with no reason given."

"If you haven't got a union, they can do just that," there was an edge of bitterness in her voice which was understandable under the circumstances.

"You want to know how Franco died? Whether there were any auspicious circumstances?"

"Suspicious, yes."

"Well I can give you suspicious circumstances by the bucket load but the evidence could be expensive. I've just lost my job after all."

Micah, who is quite good with sympathetic noises, made them to Caroline.

"Well, it's like this. I knew as how that George and Thelma had been carrying on behind Franco's back. I couldn't approve of that. When they started doing it in front of him, that was the end of him."

"How do you mean?"

She looked at me pityingly. "Snapchat of course. They sent him pictures."

"None were found on his computer."

It was Micah's turn to look pitying.

"Snapchat pictures vanish after a defined period of time and leave no trace," Micah remarked.

"You cannot take a screenshot of a snapchat as it notifies the sender. Nothing stopped me using my phone to capture some of the images. They were disgusting. I mean they were both old and that made it quite disgusting to me. Just imagine what it must have done to Mr Franco."

"They wouldn't need to jury-rig his pacemaker. These images would have been enough to give him a heart attack. Do you think he was unaware of the affair?" I asked.

"Totally. The old man was always talking about what a wonderful faithful wife he had. That was before the snapchats of course. I can let you have the evidence for a price. Tillotson has offered 2K for them but I think they are worth a good 5k of anybody's money."

"Well let me just look at them for a minute. If they are as good as you say, they are worth at least that," Micah answered.

I thought about our bank balance but a look from Micah suggested that I keep a straight face. I talked to Caroline while Micah flipped through the images on Caroline's phone. Some of them were x-rated, I noticed.

She handed the phone back to Caroline and said, "We will let you know about our price for these photos. There is still one problem. We can imagine a clever lawyer suggesting that George only intended to taunt not kill. Can you shed any light on that?"

After realising the money would be delayed, Caroline left in a huff and a taxi.

Micah actually laughed then started typing furiously on her laptop. After a brief period, she looked up and said the one word, "Yes!"

"Both the loving wife and the devoted brother had obtained information about Franco's medical condition. George even asked the doctor whether a shock would be enough to trigger what they termed a 'fatal event'. We have a case to give to Tillotson. He can do the paperwork."

"What about the pictures?"

"Oh. I copied them all to my laptop while you were chatting up that Caroline. Now how about a bottle of Cabernet Sauvignon? We have something to celebrate."

Advent in the Graveyard

"What are we doing here?" asked Micah, "It doesn't look like a crime scene, although there are bodies all over the place."

"We are interested in one in particular," I said mildly and gestured towards a gravestone.

"Thomas Shufflebottom, born 1852, fell asleep 1901," Micah read. "Forty-nine was a reasonable age in the Victorian era, 41 was the average, well it was for the Shufflebottoms of this world. The rich lived longer but it's a bit late for us to investigate that. We can't get an exhumation order for a start. Why are we interested?"

"Well it is because of that queerest of all fish, a paying customer," I said.

"Tell me more," Micah seemed interested.

"Our Thomas has a direct descendant, Sylvia Thomas. The family changed the name to Thomas in the 1930s, possibly out of respect for old Tom and possibly because they found 'Shufflebottom' only provoked amusement rather than respect when they moved down south seeking work. Sylvia's father and Tom's grandson was a Thomas Thomas who was teased as 'tomtom' by his workmates at the dairy if that's relevant."

"It isn't," said Micah shortly.

"So the Shufflebottoms had severed their connection with sheep. The name means 'sheep-well valley'..."

"I know."

"Really?"

"Well Google does, which comes to the same thing," she smiled sweetly.

I noticed Micah had her laptop on her knee.

"Can you..."

"No."

"...access the local newspaper archives?"

"Still no. The reception is quite dead here most of the time. I have GPRS."

In response to my frown, she said, "General Purpose Rubbish Signal. Now, does the Bluebell Inn have wifi?"

"Let's go and find out."

The Bluebell was decorated for Christmas. The barmaid confided that the tinsel, holly and ivy had appeared as the Halloween paraphernalia was coming down.

Micah would not conduct inquiries in a bar. She felt fairly safe from eavesdroppers in a graveyard but the live ears in a public place were a different matter. Our conversation over steak and kidney pie and a safe Merlot (I wouldn't write home about either but needs must) was about harmless topics.

After half an hour searching the local press and other available records from 1901 in our room. she started using her dark arts to look at the police records – it turned out there was nothing before the great reorganisation of 1959: nothing online at least.

"Thomas Shufflebottom did not 'fall asleep' in 1901," she concluded. "Not a bit of it. Here is a newspaper account of what happened:

'Violence came to the picturesque little village of Posset on Saturday night. A local man, Mr. Edward Sandbank, was involved in an altercation with Thomas Shufflebottom which left Mr. Sandbank with a serious knife injury. The local police acted with celerity and dispatch and Shufflebottom was arrested on the spot. The assailant, Shufflebottom, later died in police custody from injuries sustained in the fight.'

"What do you think of that?"

"At least one of 'celerity' or 'dispatch' is unnecessary."

"I don't mean the prose style of the local paper," she said patiently, "I mean the death in custody."

I sat and thought for a moment.

"He died from his injuries?"

"Yes."

"That means the police left him to die. Did he get any medical attention?"

"We don't know. Of course, medical records go back further than police records. And some of them have been put online."

"Surely they are anonymous."

"Surely indeed," Micah said, "there was a project initiated by Sheffield University to produce a collection of the medical records from Yorkshire for statistical analysis. All of the data were anonymised. And you needn't look at me like that, data is a plural."

She was typing furiously as she spoke. It was a habit of hers

"And there was one, only one, death in custody in the village of Posset. Let's call him Mr. X."

"And what do we know of the unfortunate Mr. X?" I asked.

"The official pathologist's report indicated that he hanged himself in his cell but that information was withheld so Mr. X could have a burial in St Michael's churchyard."

"Mr. X had been seen by a local doctor with the unfortunate name of Blood. His wounds were adequately dressed according to the pathologist and he certainly did not die from his injuries as the newspaper report would suggest."

We, all right, Micah, searched online for a decent restaurant in Posset. It turned out that the best, indeed the only, place to eat in Posset was the Bluebell. This was lucky as it happened.

The food was as lacklustre as it had been at lunch and the Cabernet Sauvignon which I ventured a glass of was distinctly off. We retreated to the safety of the Merlot.

The good luck came when I let slip the name of Shufflebottom in the presence of the bar staff. A muttered "Lancastrian scum." from the landlord was hastily shushed by the landlady who produced her most winning smile and confided, "You mustn't mind old grumpypants," in an undertone.

I had once worked with a colleague from Lancaster and I recalled that any amount of ribbing or downright abuse from customers would leave him unmoved. If someone erroneously suggested he was from Yorkshire, however, he went a funny colour and let out a noise similar to a steam engine under pressure.

Micah's father, the erstwhile Reverend Backhouse, had lost his faith in his fifties. He left the church. He left Micah's mother and went to live with his boyfriend in Brighton. Micah always maintained that this gave her the right to access parish records anywhere in the UK and every vicar we had met in our long career had agreed with her.

The vicar of St Michael's in Posset agreed so much that he barred me from seeing the records while Micah perused the dusty volumes in the sacristy. He engaged me in an hour of charming conversation about church architecture. Afterwards, I wished I had taken notes because he seemed to know his stuff.

After this, Micah came out of the sacristy, showered profuse thanks on the reverend and then turned to me.

"I want to tell you a story," she said in a passable imitation of Max Bygraves' brother, "In 1901 our Mr. X (who I can now definitely identify as the 'Lancastrian scum' Tom Shufflebottom) published the banns for his proposed marriage to one Amelia Cousins, spinster of this parish. What is interesting about that is that two months later, said Amelia was married to one Edward Sandbank."

"Sandbank had obviously shown enough contrition to win Amelia round in those eight short weeks," I suggested.

She held up her hand for silence.

"And just one more thing. A witness at the wedding was the brother of the groom, Sergeant Sandbank of the Posset fire and police force. We can of course only speculate but it would seem that the wars of the Roses were not over for the little village of Posset and Sergeant Sandbank finished off the job his brother had begun."

"You have earned your money for Miss Sylvia Thomas." Micah beamed.

"Well," I said, "one of us has."

The Priestly Murder

It is easy to confuse our local twittens (half-concealed footpaths) with the drive of a private house. It was after making that mistake that I came face to face with Mrs Priestly. Her home really did look like a castle and she defended it like one.

"Get off my property!" was her introduction. If she had a shotgun she would have threatened me with it.

While making a hasty retreat I noticed something which I was later to recall when its significance became clear.

A week later in the John Selden, Micah spread the *Worthing Herald* over the table. The local rag normally has to make the mundane seem interesting enough to make people buy the paper. So who can blame them for making a feast of a real murder on their patch?

The story was accompanied by an artist's impression of the young victim being bundled into the boot of a car. He was tied hand and foot. The make of car was not identified because it was one of the facts for which the police were searching.

There was also a photo of the lone plimsoll on a muddy path which had led a dog-walker to discover the body of the victim, young Mark Priestly.

The paper read,

"Eagle-eyed dog-walker Frances Cote spotted the plimsoll of Mark Priestly on the Rec at Durrington and followed the trail with her dog, Percy, to find the body of the missing thirteen-year-old schoolboy hidden inexpertly in the bushes.

"The police are seeking anyone who visited Durrington Rec or saw anything on Friday night."

"Inspector Tillotson told the *Worthing Herald,* "We are not concerned about what people were doing on the Rec on Friday night. We only want to eliminate them from our inquiries and any information which they do have could be vital. Rest assured we will soon have the name and address of everyone who visited the Rec on Friday night."

"For anyone to fail to come forward would be regarded as suspicious."

"The forensic science department has ascertained that the murderer took the body in the boot of a car to the scene. The teenager had been murdered by strangulation and it is probable that the crime was committed in a garage. Oil stains on the school uniform of the victim would seem to indicate this."

"The mother, Mrs Carla Priestly, was quoted as saying, 'I hope they catch this man before he kills any other youngsters like my darling Mark.'"

"I am sorry to say that Mrs Priestly would be at the top of my list of suspects," I said. "Apart from being a thoroughly unpleasant person..."

"Not a criminal offence," Micah added.

"Apart from that, a look at her front garden speaks volumes. Nothing lives there. There is a dead tree with a plaster bird on it. The area is paved but the bed is covered with pebbles. It is not a garden for a child. It is a garden for a child-hater," I said.

"For your sake, I will put her on my list of suspects," Micah conceded.

"Also on general principles, 'The nearer in blood the nearer bloody,'" I said.

"Malcolm?"

"Donalbain, but don't put him down as a suspect. Not yet."

More Radio took up the story the next day. A local pervert (their word) Sorlo Zamizdat who was not only on the sex offenders' register but also had a foreign-sounding name, had been grooming Mark on social media. He was 'helping police with their inquiries.'

They mentioned the name of the chatroom which Mark and Sorlo had met on. This must have sent every paedophile in a five-mile radius straight there. It also sent Micah in the same direction for different reasons.

Chatrooms are not supposed to keep a record of previous conversations. However, they are also keen to keep the police on-side. As a result, they will release the record they are not supposed to keep to the appropriate authorities while telling the punters they would never do such a thing.

Micah's shortest route to this record was via the police network. An inspector used his laptop to access the secure network which meant it was only as secure as his laptop. It leaked like a colander according to Micah and she should know.

Sorlo had got himself on the sex-offenders' register, Micah informed me, some twenty years earlier when he was eighteen and his girlfriend who (in his version of events) swore blind she was over 16, turned out to be 15 years and 11 months. He had received a custodial sentence in prison and a life-sentence of being hauled in by the police whenever a sex crime was reported. So far they had been unable to pin anything on him and they were getting frustrated.

Sorlo and Mark were identified by their IP addresses which the chatroom operators had provided. Online they used the names "Bob" and "Les".

The conversation between "Bob" and "Les" on the chatroom had gone very well. They had talked about music, living in Worthing and the TV programs they both liked. Then "Bob" had asked "Les" for his birthday. Without thinking, he had given his real birthday. At this point, "Bob" terminated the chat. As far as we could ascertain he never returned to the chatroom. The conversation had preceded the abduction and murder by three months.

The police had had to reluctantly release Sorlo with a stern warning.

We took Barker for a walk over Durrington Rec. There were police tapes in evidence but no police officers on the scene now the body had been removed. It was clear where the body had been. However, "concealed" did not describe the spot. Taking Barker back after dark we could see that the place was in complete darkness and the spot would have seemed a good hiding place to the murderer.

Micah accessed the police files. Sorlo did not possess a car. Mr Priestly, who lived in Scarborough where Mark visited him on alternate weekends, had a Rover. The police search had concentrated on the boot of the car which was untidy and not too clean. There were no traces of Mark's DNA there. There were traces in the house, explained by his fortnightly visits. There were no traces in the garage and Horace Priestly expressed surprise that the police searched there.

Mrs Priestly, and here my ears pricked up, had a Lexus with a remarkably clean boot which was empty and had been vacuumed and shampooed. There were traces of Mark's DNA in the house and in the garage. Mrs Priestly was questioned about this and explained that Mark liked to play there.

"A thirteen-year-old playing in the garage?"

"That's what she said," Micah insisted. She continued, "There was an unfortunate contretemps when the police were searching. The team were trapped in the garage and had to phone their colleagues to get out of there. There was no way to unlock the door from the inside."

I looked at Micah. She shrugged. "Yes. It would seem most likely that Mark was not 'playing' in the garage. He was imprisoned in there."

"He might have taken out his frustrations on mummy's car."

"Not if it were to be parked on the drive."

Micah was thoughtful.

"We should have a word with both parents if possible. We should start with Mr and hope he isn't as big a pain in the behind as Mrs," she concluded.

"Smell that!" was how Horace Priestly greeted us. We had to judge from his expression whether he was boasting or complaining. We jointly concluded that he was boasting and we nodded appreciatively. There was nothing to smell.

"What you can smell is Oxy-plus. It just adds enough oxygen to the air to make you more alive. It helps you to concentrate and to win at life. It improves your sex life," he gave a laugh I didn't like the sound of and added, "It's my greatest invention. It has made me a cool million so far. Now come in, come in."

The father didn't seem grief-stricken by the death of the son but grief takes us all in different ways. Our cover story was that we were from the criminal injuries compensation board because we knew they didn't make house-calls so he wouldn't have heard from them already.

"We are very sorry for your loss," Micah said.

Horace Priestly looked as though he couldn't remember what he had lost.

Then he realised. He was either a very good actor or he genuinely broke down and there were real tears.

"I am sorry, Mr Priestly," Micah had on her sympathetic smile, "but we have to ask a few questions. We will be as brief as possible."

Recovering himself, he said, "I am forgetting my manners. You have had a long journey. Can I offer you a cup of tea or something stronger?"

"I'm driving," I said, "I would love a cup of tea."

"Well if it is no bother, do you have any WKD?"

I kept the astonishment out of my face as best I could as Horace went to the kitchen and fetched a bottle of the disgusting blue alcopop from the fridge. Micah did her best to look as though she were enjoying it. Horace didn't have to fake his enjoyment of his glass of Laphroaig.

He claimed that Mark enjoyed his time staying with his dad. There was no sign of any significant other around the place. Mr Priestly seemed wholly consumed by his business interests but he did say two things which surprised us.

"Mark was keen on moving up here with me, you know. I had a spare room. The local school is quite good, I think. I quizzed him about moving away from his friends and he made a face. Perhaps he didn't have many friends."

We asked about the probable night of the murder.

"We have to ask these questions," I added.

"Well blow me down. The police already asked. I was at a business meeting in Birmingham about the launch of Oxy-plus. There were about 155 people there. It is a very hot property right now with the interest in lifestyle choices."

He went on for some time about Oxy-plus and its supposed benefits but I don't have to bore you with them. I was quite bored enough myself.

On the long journey home I asked Micah, "WKD?"

"Craig, can you imagine Horace enjoying a glass of WKD?"

"Hardly."

"Exactly. It was Mark who was drinking the revolting stuff. I know he was 13 but think back to what you were drinking then."

"Cider and Light Ale."

"Welcome to the 21st Century, Craig!"

I chickened out of any further conversation with Mrs Priestly and it as well I did because Micah made one of the major finds of the case while interviewing her about possible compensation for her criminal injuries.

Mrs Priestly was suspicious of Micah but the prospect of £4000 compensation got her attention and she was happy to give all the details for the form Micah had to fill in. She designed the form herself but it was headed "Criminal Injuries Compensation".

Micah had to use the upstairs toilet and took the opportunity to look in Mark's room. It had been tidied almost to destruction but Micah is the doyen of hiding-places. The carpet was fitted so there was no likelihood of anything under that. The wardrobe had a strip of carpet and, she discovered, a loose floorboard underneath. An exercise book with the word "Diary" on the front was underneath with some cigarettes and a small amount of money.

Micah quickly put everything back the way it was. As soon as she was home, we examined the diary together.

"I am a disappointment to my mother. She has worked so hard to give me everything and I have repaid her by being lazy and selfish. That is what The Witch said when she found the cigarettes anyway and I knew what was coming. I was locked in the garage for an hour. She put a disgusting canvas bag over my head but the first thing I did when she left me was take it off. I am used to hours alone in the garage anyway so it is a crap punishment."

"When The Witch found out her smelly canvas bag had been removed she was furious. She left me tied to a chair in the garage from then on. There was a smoky old paraffin stove. I complained about the smell and lack of oxygen. 'You like to smoke, you selfish little shit. And you don't deserve oxygen.' There was a lot more but I can't be bothered to write it down."

Mrs Priestly was routinely called "The Witch" with capital letters and the diary recorded how the punishments had become worse. Mark had been locked in the boot of the car, tied up with rubber hoses. Nothing that would leave any marks so he heeded "The Witch's" warning not to tell any of the authorities at school.

"The Witch" had responded particularly badly to the news that Mr Priestly was prepared to take Mark. Apparently, she "went ballistic" but the diary did not give details of what form this took.

"Your hunch..." Micah began.

"Evidence..."I said.

"Hunch," Micah insisted, "anyway it seems your intuition if you prefer that word, was right. She is a child-hater. The diary is evidence enough for a charge of imprisonment and mistreating a minor. It is not evidence of murder. We hand the diary over to the police."

"And tell them how we got it?" I asked.

"Perhaps we received it in the post. The envelope wound up in the trash? Something along those lines. The police need this."

I agreed.

"They will have her in for questioning anyway."

Our next move was discussed over a rather nice Merlot and we decided it was worth having a chat with Mark's teacher, Mr Stanhope.

The classroom took me back further then I care to remember. Schooldays were not entirely joyful for me. One innovation was the lingering smell of Lynx. In my day a boys' classroom smelt of boy. This was a marginal improvement.

Mr Stanhope came in to see us and I felt instinctively he was about to send me off to the head for six of the best. Fortunately, he wasn't.

"Mark Priestly? He was a quiet lad and didn't get in trouble. I smelt tobacco on him at times but these days you have to be pleased if it isn't something stronger."

He gave a laugh which went nowhere.

"As I say, he was withdrawn but never showed any signs of injury or physical neglect," he sighed, "The trouble is there are other kinds of injury, other kinds of neglect. We do our best for our boys but a good school can't wash away the problems of an unhappy home."

"The parents came to parents' evenings separately. The mother wanted him to do well and would make sure he wasn't happy if he didn't. The father, from what he said, wanted him to be happy so he could do well. Talking to them was like being on the receiving end of a 'good cop bad cop' routine."

"All of the staff and of course his classmates were traumatised by the murder. One in particular, Tony Brantling. You will need his parents' say-so to talk to him but it would be worthwhile."

"If you can catch the person who did this, I will be eternally grateful. Good luck," were his parting words.

We explained to the Brantlings that we were from Thompsons Press. We didn't explain that Thompsons Press haven't published newspapers for a decade.

We said that we couldn't pay for information but we thought that Tony would do whatever he could to help catch Mark's killer.

"He doesn't know anything, I'm afraid," Mrs Brantling was doubtful.

"He might not know how important his knowledge is," I suggested.

"I'll see what he says."

Mrs Brantling bustled off like the PA to a senior statesman to see if the great man could see us. It seemed he could.

Tony came in. He didn't look either of us in the face and plonked himself down on the sofa. He was a boy of Mark's age and had a fine incipient teenage attitude about him.

"Anything you tell us about Mark might help us to catch his killer."

"The Witch killed him. That's what he used to call his passive-aggressive mother."

"The thing is, Tony, our readers are going to need evidence."

Tony detailed some of the things Mrs Priestly had done to Mark as Mark himself had put in his diary. Stroppy teenager though he was, Tony had been a good listener for Mark. It was evidence of an attitude and it was evidence of mistreatment certainly, not murder.

Then he let slip an interesting fact.

"On that last day, Mark took the afternoon off school. It was only Maths and his dad was coming down from Scarborough."

"Thank you, Tony. You have been very helpful."

As we walked Barker that evening, Micah made arrangements over the telephone to visit Mr Priestly to discuss a discrepancy in his evidence.

"I am sure we can sort all of this out between us," Micah said.

"Yes of course," he replied.

When we got to Scarborough, it was a very deflated Mr Priestly we met. When I asked why he had lied to us about his movements on the day of the murder, he looked as though he would break down in tears again. He didn't answer for a long moment.

"I was in Crawley to promote Oxy-Plus on that day so it was a short trip to Worthing and a long one to Birmingham but I had had an urgent phone call from Mark. He wanted me to take him away immediately. I couldn't ignore it."

"Carla was in the kitchen when I arrived and she was suspiciously calm. 'You have come to collect Mark, no doubt. You can find him in the garage.' was all she said.

He paused.

"You already know what I found in the garage." There was a plea in his tone.

"If you please, Mr Priestly,"

"He was dead. She had strangled him with her own hands. She wore rubber gloves, she boasted to me. There would be no evidence to prove it was her. And now I had come to her door conveniently and even gone into the garage like a fool, I would be the suspect if I didn't get out and never return."

"I didn't know what to think. I drove to Birmingham under automatic pilot I suppose."

"And talked enthusiastically about Oxy-Plus?" Micah asked.

He nodded. "I'm not proud of myself..."

"I couldn't care less," said Micah, "You know you have to take this evidence to the police straight away."

"But..."

"But nothing," I said. "You are a key witness in a murder case and if you go on withholding evidence you will become a suspect."

When the case came to court it dragged on for weeks and there wasn't much of the Priestly dirty washing the public didn't know about by the end. Although the diary did not constitute evidence of murder, it did tip the balance of probability towards "The Witch." She got a long term in prison rather than a public burning though.

Death's Calling Card

I have never understood why Micah gets so agitated whenever the ace of spades comes into play when we indulge in the occasional game of rummy at the John Selden. We never play for money because pubs need to be licensed for that sort of thing.

"It's death's calling card," she once explained.

"It's superstitious nonsense," I thought, but refrained from saying.

Perhaps that was just as well because we were to encounter Micah's least favourite card in the most macabre of circumstances.

The Smithson family were a macabre lot at the best of times. I knew them slightly as neighbours but Micah is what an impolite person might call nosy, which is no bad thing for a detective of course.

So it was that Micah was the first person Carmen Smithson rang when tragedy struck. I will mention now that her mother did not name her after the heated rollers. This was, Carmen insisted, "a joke." I leave you to judge.

"We will come round straight away," Micah said.

Turning to me, she added, "I will tell them they should call the police when we have had a look at the crime scene."

"And to touch nothing?"

"Quite," Micah gave me a look which said she was not a complete imbecile.

Anatole and Carmen Smithson and their grown-up son, Gregory who still lived with them at the age of 38 had been playing cards with a friend of the family, Bernard Cash.

Anatole had died where he sat. With a "strangled sort of noise," he had dropped his cards and cashed in his chips so to speak. I noticed he had been holding the eights of spades and clubs, the ace of clubs and our old nemesis the ace of spades. The other players had left their cards where they were. While the family called for medical assistance (which proved to be a futile exercise) I took a glance at the other hands and realised that Anatole's cards were winning ones. He also had an ace of diamonds in the hole, which clinched the matter.

Micah looked at the cards with a kind of superstitious dread.

"That is a dead man's hand," she confided.

"So I see," I said.

She sighed. "It is called a dead man's hand because according to legend it was the hand Bill Hickok had when he was shot dead. It is very unlucky," she held up her hand, "even when it is a winning hand."

I held my tongue. It had certainly been unlucky for Anatole Smithson that night.

We prevailed upon Mr Cash to remain although he seemed keen not to meet the police. He explained this, with a laugh, "I am a victim of nominal determinism. With a name like Cash, people assume they can come to me for help when they need a little more money."

"And what rate of interest do you charge?" Micah asked sweetly.

"Well I don't like to talk about that kind of thing, Mrs McLairy but I can tell you it is a lot less than those gangsters at Wonga." He laughed again.

"Such as..."

"I suppose it works out at about, you know, in rough figures 999 percent APR. Nothing which people can't afford." He looked at Carmen and the look on her face suggested that Bernard Cash was not so much a family friend as a creditor.

While the family were waiting for the police to arrive we had a chance to look at the dining room where they had been playing cards before joining them in the living room. The first thing was obvious. There was a smell in the air which ex-smokers find nauseating. It would linger for a long time.

I have never read a monograph about 100 types of cigarette ash but fortunately, Anatole smoked Sobranie as a rule and the distinctive gold filter tips and black paper indicated that he had smoked three of them. Bernard and Carmen were non-smokers or at least had no ashtrays. Gregory, it seemed, was a nervous smoker so he left half the cigarette in the ash-tray with the words "Players No 6" quite clear. It seemed he had less expensive tastes than his father.

What was missing were cups and glasses. It seems that despite the death of a family member, someone had had the foresight to put them in the dishwasher. Valuable evidence had been destroyed.

There was something else we noticed. When we had played cards with the Smithsons on a previous occasion, there had been six upright chairs in the room around the table. There were now four. When we went into the living room to join the family waiting for the police the two chairs were awkwardly placed against the wall.

The conversation did not exactly flow. Carmen was distraught. Cash was trying to get her to "buck up" and "grow some" until Micah intervened with tea and sympathy. Gregory was sitting morosely in a corner smoking, every inch the surly teenager.

This left me with Bernard. His conversation consisted entirely of football. The fact I know nothing and care less about watching 22 millionaires ruin a lawn did not deter him. He kept up a steady stream of talk which I let wash over me. The polite smile was wearing a little thin by the time the police arrived.

Inspector Tillotson was not exactly pleased to see us but it is just possible our presence caused him to put on a show of efficiency. He gave the room a cursory once-over and then left it to his forensic team who were more properly dressed for that sort of thing.

He seemed surprised to see Cash.

"Hello, Bernard. Grace not with you tonight?"

"No, Ben, she's washing her hair tonight. You know what women are like."

The two exchanged smiles. In my experience, Ben Tillotson is only on such terms of camaraderie with other police officers and known criminals.

"Washing her hair" seemed a thin excuse.

I was pleased to note from Ben's conversation with his colleagues his view of Dr Winter, or 'the old windbag' as he put it, was on a par with mine. He would be giving the task of the post-mortem to another expert. It would be someone younger and fitter (and less of a windbag) than Dr Winter. Winter's Death Certificate might not be worth the paper it was written on.

He wanted to interview Carmen alone but he was actually not displeased to have Micah along as a chaperone or perhaps a responsible adult.

Micah is very responsible but she does have the habit of recording all her conversations on the telephone without the knowledge of the other participants.

Ben Tillotson then interviewed us. He turned to Bernard and left Gregory to last. I silently wished him luck with that.

His sergeant then took our addresses and warned us sternly not to leave the country without informing them.

When we got home, Micah played me the recording.

"Can you tell us in your own words what happened?"

"We were just having a friendly game of whist. There was just my son Gregory, Bernard, Anatole and myself."

"It looked like poker to me," Micah said quietly.

"What the hell does it matter?" Carmen screeched. When it comes to screeching, Carmen is right up there with the owls.

There was a silence.

"We were playing poker, whist, whatever, happy families. Anatole gave a strangled sort of noise and collapsed as you can see. Bernard felt his neck for a pulse but there was none. He was..." She left the sentence unfinished.

"Are there usually six chairs in the room?"

"What the hell have you been taking, Micah? What the hell does it matter how many chairs there were? My husband, my husband is...oh it's terrible. What will Gregory do without a father? What will I do without...really Micah you can stick the chairs up your..."

The recording stopped at that point and then continued with all the routine questions Tillotson could think of. At the end, he said quietly to Micah, "Is there anything you can find out about the family's finances? Nobody invited Bernard Cash into their house voluntarily if you know what I mean. Use your dark arts, Mrs McLairy, use your dark arts for an old friend."

We both laughed at the old bigot's description of himself but Micah wasted no time using her dark arts on the Smithson's bank account. She knew which bank Anatole used because he was old-fashioned enough to make deposits in person at the Nationwide in Goring. A user can access their own account with a pin number. Thousands are unwise enough to use their own date of birth. Anatole was one of them.

"This is grim reading. The money goes out faster than it comes in. Cash in and cash out. It is very like the account of a gambler who keeps losing and losing. The sums he loses are seldom whole hundreds or whole thousands. The deposits frequently are. I would run the account numbers past old Ben Tillotson but as I said they are all in cash. Our kindly local moneylender likes to live up to his name."

"The Smithson family were up that well-known creek without the benefit of a paddle?" I asked.

Micah nodded.

She took a sip of her mushroom and nettle tea, followed by a face which spoke volumes about her choice of a healthy beverage.

I poured it down the sink and poured her a hearty glass of Cabernet Sauvignon while she found another chink in the armour of the police computer system. After a while, she sat back, took a sip from her glass and said,

"They have given the post-mortem to someone who can be trusted to write his own name so there ought to be some hope there. Tillotson has gone home for the night because the PM isn't until tomorrow morning and the death is not yet "suspicious."

"The police have had their eye on the creepy Mr Cash for some time. His interest rates are daylight robbery but there are a number of companies which advertise quite openly on the television which charge more. I doubt if they have quite the same persistence of enforcement as Mr Cash but nothing has been proved to the satisfaction of the Crown Prosecution Service as yet."

"Grace Cash, his common-law wife, had even less reason to be keen to see the police than Bernard. She has a string of convictions stretching from petty larceny to actual bodily harm, the latter is understandable since it was committed on Mr Cash himself. There is nothing in the last four years. I ,mean there is nothing for which she has been prosecuted but there is a suspicion that she is one of Bernard's less unpleasant enforcers.

"Greg has an unexceptional record with a couple of drunk and disorderly charges when he was a teenager, a real teenager that is, not the overgrown lump he has become. You will not be surprised to know that he has no visible means of financial support."

"Anatole, as you know, had a job with a local shop. They speak very highly of him and think it will be hard to find someone with such a good work ethic..."

"Willing to work for peanuts?" I suggested.

Micah nodded.

"Are there any details of the allegations against Mr Cash's nasty enforcer?" I asked.

"None of Mr Cash's debtors croaked as far as I know and all of them lived to withdraw their statements. However, one of the allegations seems to have been of a more personal nature. It was withdrawn but it came from a woman that Grace thought was playing fast and loose with Bernard."

I waited.

"Her name is Marsha Marshall improbably, Marshall might be her married name. We could have a word with her tomorrow. Now is there another glass in that bottle?"

"No."

"I am sure there is another bottle."

"Fancy some mushroom and nettle tea?"

Micah threw a cushion at me.

Marsha Marshall met us at the door wearing a pink housecoat and an absolutely horrific green face mask which Boots told her would improve her looks.

"Ms Marshall?"

"Mrs," she said sharply, cracking the face mask around the lips so it looked slightly more grotesque.

"We are following up the incident involving Mrs Cash," Micah said, taking out a notepad.

"I have nothing to say about that."

"You might be due for compensation," Micah added.

"You'd better come in."

We sat down in the living room. Micah was unphased by the face mask. Apparently, it needed to stay on for twenty more minutes.

After a while, Mrs Marshall said, "That bitch was careful not to leave no marks. She came in here shouting about how I'd seduced her husband. Well I didn't know Bernard, he called hisself John but then a lot of men do, was married and he paid good money.

"On top of that, when I complained to the filth, pardon me, the police, she came back and threatened me family."

I looked around the room. There was no sign that Marsha had children.

Seeing the look, she said, "I mean she said she knew someone who could go round and burn down me parents' house with no questions asked. I believed her."

So did I.

"So no compensation?" Beneath the mask, it was hard to see how she felt about anything.

"Well, we'll have to see," Micah was non-committal, "Thank you for your time."

When we got home, there was news.

More Radio said, "Police are investigating the suspicious death of local shopkeeper, Anatole Smithson. Mr Smithson's post-mortem revealed that he had been injected with a fatal dose of insulin. This overturned a conclusion of 'natural causes' reached by a local doctor."

"We have Mr Smithson's son, Gregory, on the line."

"Mr Smithson, this must have come as a shock to you."

"I couldn't say. Well yes if you say so."

"What sort of a man was your father?"

"I don't really know. I mean he was my father so I loved him, whatever that means."

"Thank you, Mr Smithson."

Micah was busy on her laptop. That did not stop her commenting, "That is the longest sentence anyone has ever got out of Greg. I see they have promoted Anatole from shop assistant to shopkeeper."

"Now look. The post-mortem showed a trace of insulin but it occurs naturally in the body. It led the pathologist to search for a needle site. It was inside Anatole's nose. He didn't have diabetes and in any case, nobody injects themselves up the nose so foul play was suspected."

"And this took place while they were playing cards?" I asked.

Micah made a snorting noise which translates as "Come off it!"

Barker always barked when she did this and he lived up to his reputation.

"No. Whatever else the Smithsons and their friends got up to, they were not playing cards."

Micah always uses an old-fashioned notebook for lists of suspects. She wrote down,

"Anatole Smithson

Carmen Smithson

Gregory Smithson

Bernard Cash

Grace Cash"

She then neatly bracketed them together.

I queried the first item on the list.

"We must not overlook the possibility that Anatole was overwhelmed by his debts and decided to take his own life. The unusual method of his suicide could be a way that would enable Carmen to claim on his insurance if it were not detected."

"How do you know about the insurance?

"Regular payments from his Nationwide Policy."

"And they are all bracketed together because they must all have been involved in setting up the fake card game?" I asked.

Micah nodded.

"So if they were all involved, who is the weakest link?"

"There are two, the two surviving Smithsons. Grace and Bernard are used to being questioned and they will have their stories off pat. I don't want to tip them off either."

I was not sanguine about getting anything beyond a grunt out of Greg so it was time to offer tea and sympathy to Carmen.

That morning *More Radio* was full of a new story. "The body of a homeless woman has been found in one of the seafront shelters on the promenade at Worthing seafront. These seafront shelters, commonly known as "tramps' hotels" locally were a haunt of homeless people and a body could remain undetected there for some time. The woman has not as yet been identified by the police. A Sussex Police spokesman is on the line."

"Thank you for helping us with this inquiry. You know, identity among the indigent population is nebulous. Homeless people will not necessarily know or remember the name of someone else who is in the same predicament. And so it has proved in this case. None of the homeless people we interviewed were able to put a name to this face. It may be hard to find out who this poor woman was. She had clearly been dead for two days at least. The picture will be on our website and the local newspapers will be offered it. If any member of the public can identify her we urge them to come forward."

This was not relevant to our case, or so we thought. How wrong we were.

Carmen was actually wearing heated rollers when we arrived. Micah looked at me. I looked at Micah. We made no comment.

"Do come in, it's nice to see a friendly face. Micah, I'm sorry if I was a bit sharp with you the other night but I was so upset about … you know."

"Of course, Carmen. I quite understand. It's just that lying to the police is a very serious matter."

"Micah, how can you possibly..."

"The game of cards, Carmen?" I asked quietly.

Carmen was silent while she thought about that.

"And the chairs." I added, "even the smallest discrepancy in your account will make the police suspicious."

When she had had time to think about this, Micah said, "Why don't you just tell us what really happened and we can decide between us what to tell the police?"

"I daren't. I owe him so much money!"

"Bernard Cash?"

Carmen nodded.

"Well tell us the truth and shame the devil."

"He is the devil!"

"Not a family friend then?" I asked. Micah gave me a look. I said no more.

After a little more coaxing (Micah could coax for England if it were an Olympic sport) Carmen began talking. Once she had started she seemed to draw confidence from the fact she was telling the truth for once. The lies had been choking her.

"The chairs, you would go on about those bloody chairs, Micah. And in a way you were right. There were only four chairs because the police were not to know how many of us there were. The card game was set up. Bernard seemed to take pleasure in the cards he had put in Anatole's hand. He laughed."

"He laughed!" she repeated as if realising how awful that was for the first time.

"Anatole had been sleeping in the lounge. The rest of us had been having a quiet drink in here. I remember Grace went in but it was only for a minute. She wore rubber gloves but one doesn't like to inquire. Bernard came in and announced quite calmly that Anatole had died in his sleep. 'So all his debt is yours now, Carmen. We can discuss how to pay it.'"

Then Grace came in and shouted at him, 'She will pay it in bloody cash, not in your bed!'"

'Now, Grace, I think you had better go home,' he said."

"Then after a while, he persuaded her that it was best if she didn't stay and talk with the police. That was when he got Greg to move the chairs."

I was amazed anyone could get Greg to do anything and my look probably betrayed that thought because Carmen talked about how persuasive Bernard could be.

"If you tell the police then it will be your word against Bernard's and it will not look good that you didn't tell them straight away. Say you were terrified of what he might do if you grassed on him, something like that." Micah looked at me.

"And Craig and I will see if we can get any evidence on persuasive Bernard."

Micah's cover story of choice was that we wanted to take out a loan at extortionate interest because we were in dire straits financially. The second part of that was true but we had not taken leave of our senses enough to trust ourselves to Mr Cash.

It turned out that "persuasive Bernard" was unlikely to be persuaded. At least we couldn't do so. A tearful Grace came to the door. Somehow her voice seemed familiar but it took me a while to put two and two together.

"I've called the ambulance. I think he's had a heart attack."

We didn't. It was too much of a coincidence. Bernard was no longer among the living and I called the police on my mobile while Micah was keeping Grace talking.

It wasn't old Ben Tillotson on the case but the police had utilised the services of Dr Latimer since it dawned on them that Dr Winter wasn't exactly competent to tie his own shoelaces. It didn't take Latimer too long to come to the conclusion that the same method had been used for both murders.

"I've been looking into Grace's employment records," Micah confided, "she had a brief career as a cleaner at the local hospital. Nothing was proved of course but a number of things went missing, rubber gloves, class A drugs, some syringes and an unquantifiable amount of guess what?"

I didn't have to say, 'insulin' but I did anyway.

Old Ben turned up on our doorstep the next day.

"Mr McLairy, Mrs McLairy oh and Barker, how are you, boy?"

He ruffled Barker's fur and gave him something out of his pocket – a fluff-covered treat but Barker was not fussy.

He showed us a photograph.

"Do you know this woman?"

We looked hard but were unable to identify her.

"So you can't identify her as Marsha Marshall?"

"Miss Marshall was in the middle of a facial treatment when we saw her two days ago... " I began.

"No, she wasn't. She was a corpse in a seafront shelter. Her days of facials were over."

"You mean?"

"I'm afraid the Durrington Detective Agency has made a complete Horlicks of this one. The woman you saw must have been her killer and we have every reason to suspect she was Grace Cash."

Tillotson looked smug, though in his case it is hard to tell the difference.

"She arranged the murder of Anatole Smithson and Marsha Marshall and then she used the exact same method to dispose of the odious Cash. Apparently, she was only after his money. Now how about a cup of tea?"

Old Ben was coaxed into swapping the tea for a glass of Black Shiraz and we settled down to an evening of reminiscences. These mainly consisted of him pointing out the various errors of our ways. We did not play cards.

Once in a Blue Moon

"It's a rare occurrence, like two full moons in the same month," I explained.

"Or it's the new Chinese Restaurant in Goring," Micah replied.

Goring lies between Durrington on Sea and the sea. Historians believe that once the boundaries were drawn differently or perhaps Goring was underwater. We decided to venture out of our comfort zone for once and give the new restaurant a try.

Micah has the unfortunate habit of listening to the conversations of other diners. It is no bad thing for a detective to be a bit on the nosy side and I have to admit the couple were having a strange conversation.

The man in the leather jacket looked to be in his mid-thirties. The woman wore an identical leather jacket and in every respect, she seemed to be trying hard to look like her companion. They both had fair hair and it was cut to a similar length. He had a collection of rings which would prove useful in a bare-knuckle fight and so did she. She drew the line at the beard, however. We were to find their names were Jack Edson and Jackie Dubson but that was after matters unfolded to a tragic conclusion.

"I am going to give you such a thrashing," Jack said conversationally.

"You mean like you did at canasta?" Jackie asked with a laugh.

"That was a fluke."

"Oh yes of course. And tell me, Jack, just how is this 'thrashing' going to be administered?"

"Anything you like. Pitch and putt, crazy golf, tiddlywinks..."

"No crazy golf. You always beat me at that. I think it must be because you are crazy. And you don't mean tiddlywinks because you don't even know the rules."

"Yes, I do."

"You don't. You lost because you squidged a wink that was squodged and the rules clearly state..."

"Your rules perhaps."

"No I mean the rules. Anyway forget that nonsense. Pitch and putt it is. Tomorrow at Marine Gardens. Be there."

They drifted off into a more normal girl-meets-boy conversation and Micah lost interest. The conversation was one we were to recall two days later, however.

More Radio broke the news, "a body has been discovered in local beauty spot Marine Gardens. At first the body was wrongly assumed to be that of a local administrator John Edson, usually known as Jack. It was even identified as such by a close friend, Mr Lesley Norman. Mr Norman is on the line:"

"You could have knocked me down with a feather when they told me it wasn't Jack. Jack has been missing for a day. It was a woman, for Christ's sake. You could have knocked me down..."

"Thank you, Mr Norman. The police have now identified the body as one Emily Dubson who had adopted the name Jackie during the last month. The cause of death has not been established but Dr Winter has provisionally named the cause as..."

"Heart failure," we said in unison, blocking out the exact same words from More Radio.

"We need to have a word with Mr Leslie Norman," Micah said.

"To find out why he is lying?" I asked.

Micah nodded and proceeded to find out the address of Mr Norman on her phone. It was in a row of gently decaying terraced houses in Salvington Road.

"Mr Norman, we would like to offer you condolences on the death of your friend," Micah addressed the scruffy youth whose trousers seemed to have had a difference of opinion with a carving knife. He immediately started making a fuss of Barker which meant he went up in my estimation.

"Well," he had a surprisingly polite manner, "that is very kind of you but in fact I believe my friend, Jack, to be alive and well. I didn't know the junkie at all."

"Jackie Dudson?"

"Jackie, Emily, whatever. I am sorry she died from her addiction but I didn't know her."

"So the two of them were not an item?" Micah asked.

He actually laughed. "Really, I can't imagine she would be Jack's type. Good for a bit of how's yer father I expect but I doubt if they were an item. He didn't go for heroin chicks."

"I'm sorry I'm a bit lost here," (I impersonated a doddery old timer, Micah says I do it far too well), "You have mentioned twice about Ms Dudson being hooked on heroin but the official cause of death was a heart attack."

"Oh. Didn't you hear on the radio? I expect you call it the wireless, grandad. (I was going off this young man rapidly). The police are now saying that she died from an overdose of heroin. They said she didn't have any needle marks but that only means she took it by other methods."

"You identified her body as Jack's though."

"So? What about it?"

"Had she grown a beard?"

"No, my friend," he said in a despicably patronising tone, "what you don't know is this: Jack was a fanatical cyclist. In fact he was a fanatical everything. Yesterday, no the day before now, he shaved off all his body hair, all of it, because he had read somewhere that it could shave fractions of a second off his times."

As we walked Barker over Durrington rec, Micah mused, she was ticking off points on her fingers, "We know she had no track marks. I looked at her hands and they were not the hands of a smoker and her eyes were all wrong. The light was romantic in the restaurant and she had largish pupils not pinpricks but more than that, she did not strike me as a heroin addict."

"How many do you know?"

She brushed the question aside.

"I know enough to realise that young lady was very much on the ball and anyone taking heroin would lack that mental acuity. You realise what this means?"

"We have a murder on our hands and Jack Edson, the missing administrator, is the most likely suspect. You remember he was going to give her a thrashing?"

Micah nodded absent-mindedly, "That's just a figure of speech. I thrashed you at rummy last night in case you've forgotten.

That evening we were having a drink in the John Selden when an unexpected bonus arrived in the form of Detective Inspector Tillotson. Old Ben thought it only right that I should buy him a drink and he opted for Harveys. I think it is only when there is no alternative that he will condescend to drink something as poncey as wine.

"It is Micah I have come to talk to," he said as he began to down his pint in short order. "It is about this."

He put a memory stick on the table.

"When we got to Ms Edson's flat it seems it has been done over. There was a power supply for a laptop but the laptop itself had been stolen. The thief had failed to take this. This is just a copy of course. The boffins have the original (he actually called them boffins) and they are pulling out what little hair they have left over it. It seems all the files are in code."

"Encrypted," said Micah.

Old Ben is always amazed that a female knows more than he does but he was content to be lectured by Micah.

"If something is in code it cannot be broken. 'The Geese are flying south this winter" might mean we are dropping arms tonight, we are invading tomorrow or..."

"The geese are flying south this winter?" Ben ventured with a grin.

Micah nodded. "An encryption or a cypher can be broken. It just takes time. The Enigma cypher was broken because German operators were in love with the phrase 'Heil Hitler' and that sequence of letters was used often to test the machines. There was a whole lot of work to be done after that of course."

"I am not supposed to let this out of my sight. I have a feeling I might leave it on this table by accident though. How long will you need?"

"It will take as long as it takes," said Micah enigmatically, "but it could tell us a lot about Jackie/Emily. What do you know already?"

"She was adopted by a local family, the Dubsons after a troubled childhood. We are looking for her original records but Lambeth Social Services have other priorities, so they say. Curiously, the missing John Edson was also adopted by the Edson family but we cannot find any more information about him for the same reason."

"They were both from Lambeth originally," I said.

Old Ben nodded, his face said that Lambeth was one of the less pleasant suburbs of Hell.

"And then there is the obsession they developed about looking alike. That isn't normal. Not to the extent to which they took it. We think it is mutual. John removed all his body hair except what he had on top anyway. Of course, Jackie is like Jack and neighbours say that she used the name of Jack Edson. It is only your evidence from the Blue Moon that told us they must be two different people."

"What about occupations?"

"Jack was the only one with a job. He was an administrator in the National Health Service. They are more common than nurses. Jackie had no visible means of support."

Micah had said that it would take time to decrypt the files on the memory stick. I expected her to be busy for hours on end. To my surprise, she just left the laptop plugged in and switched on for the best part of 24 hours. The screen was blank. After that time it gave an alarm and the word "Warmer" came up in white lettering. Then it came up with the same word in red and finally the word "CRACKED" filled the screen.

The job had all been completed with a free-to-download app available on the internet. It was probably not exactly legal but Micah was, after all, helping the police with their inquiries.

She had opened up an Aladdin's Cave of information. We scrolled through the photographs. There were a series of selfies which showed Emily's gradual transformation into a facsimile of John Edson.

Her browsing history, apart from a very active Facebook account, Twitter and Amazon, had a search on Google for "how-to-steal-an-identity-in-seven-easy-steps". By default her gmail account was that of John Edson, her old college email address (actually we found out it was his old college) was jedson@ucl.com and the bank account was that of, I imagine you can guess the rest. She had got the bank to send her an email to change her password, gmail had sent her an email to change her gmail password to the old college email and the college had let her change the email password because she knew the address, date of birth and (adoptive) mother's maiden name for her victim.

In John Edson's name she had queried Lambeth Social Services for the name of his birth mother. She had received the answer to that question on the very day she died.

"Pure heroin can be smoked or snorted or made into suppositories. There is no evidence here that she intended to kill herself. Yet she did receive a massive overdose. Conclusion?" Micah raised an eyebrow.

"She knew her attacker very very well," I ventured.

Micah waited.

"John Edson found out about her attack on his bank account? How much was in it?"

"£280," said Micah.

"People have been killed for less," I said.

"I don't think that was all of it. She seemed obsessed with taking over his identity not just his £280. She went to great efforts because she was female and he was male. Still they did look very similar to begin with, judging from her photo gallery. So what the inquiry to Lambeth might have shown was..." Micah began.

"That they were brother and sister." I said, "did they have the same date of birth?"

"Exactly."

"To kill your twin must be like killing yourself. What do you think has happened to the real John Edson?" I asked.

"That is what we need to find out."

In the car on our trip to Croydon, I asked Micah if we knew the name of the mother of the twins. By way of reply, she started humming 'Lara's theme'.

"It's a Mrs Zhivago?"

She smiled, "no".

"Mrs Pasternak?"

"Yes. She reverted to her maiden name when her husband rode off into the sunset and left her holding the babies in 1988. She wanted to have them adopted but insisted they should be taken as a pair. Social Services tried their best but eventually accommodated them separately with families in Worthing. Their casework officers had so many clients they could scarcely keep track of the ones in Lambeth let alone out of town. The workload hasn't got any better, it would seem."

"What were they called?"

"Pavel and Petra."

"She named her after the Blue Peter dog?"

"More likely after Saint Peter. That 'Petra' was a distant memory in 1988."

"Do we suppose that Pavel/John made his way back to Croydon?"

"It is as good a place to start as any. Mrs Pasternak must know something after all."

The house was a former council house in Thornton Heath. It had been sold off by the council twenty years previously and that was the last time any repairs had been done. At a guess, that was the last time any gardening had gone on too.

When Mrs Pasternak answered the door we didn't have to tell her we had bad news for her. It was the face of someone who had had nothing but bad news all her life.

"I'm afraid we have bad news for you about Pavel," said Micah.

"Pavel?" the look of confusion on her face told us all we needed to know. She had been expecting bad news about Petra.

"You knew Petra was dead?" I said.

Mrs Pasternak started sobbing gently but she nodded.

"And you know who killed her?"

She nodded again.

"I can tell you that an Inspector Tillotson and his lads are coming here with the brief to "tear this place apart" until they find Pavel. Can we talk to him before they get here?"

She went to the staircase and shouted. She essayed 'Pavel' twice then switched to 'Jack.' When he came downstairs, mother and son embraced.

"You've been in touch for some time," I guessed.

"Five years," said Jack over the head of his mother. "I really loved Jackie. She was funny and quirky of course but I loved her. We were going to be married but that was just a dream. We tried to look alike. At first it was just a game, for me anyway.

"Then when we met at Marine Gardens she taunted me with all the information she had found out about me and about her being me as far as my bank was concerned. She boasted that I couldn't access any of my online identities."

"She treated it as a big joke even when she found out we had the same mother. She talked about Siegmund and Sieglinde and how romantic Wagner was. It was too much for me and I."

He stopped and continued after a few seconds.

"I killed her in the heat of the moment."

"With a fatal dose of heroin you just happened to have with you.?" Micah asked.

Jack just looked at us.

It was at that point that a cacophony of sirens heralded the arrival of old Ben Tillotson and his 'lads'.

Jack then tried to run but that was quite difficult to do with Micah and I holding his wrists to the arms of the chair.

"That was quite an unusual case," Micah conceded on the long drive back.

I opened my mouth.

"And if you say 'once in a blue moon' you may have to walk back," she added sweetly.

I closed my mouth again.

The Courtyard of Shadows

"It had always been called the courtyard of shadows by pupils at the school. It was north-facing and by chance or design, it was almost invariably in shadow. On midsummer's day, a shaft of light lit up the sacrificial victim before the knife was plunged into..." Micah began.

"Micah, have you been overindulging in Druid rituals again?"

"Well perhaps a little but it is a bit dark and there has been a murder. An eighteen-year-old former pupil has been stabbed. The murder took place as close to midsummer's day as makes no difference."

She put the *Worthing Herald* down on the table, took a satisfying swig of Shiraz and then continued to read.

"Dr Winter was called in by the school and for once decided it wasn't heart failure. With a ruddy great knife protruding from the victim's chest he surmised it was stabbing. The head teacher, Mr Lawson, has been keen to reassure parents that their darlings are unlikely to be stabbed on the premises. He emphasised that the victim, a Karl Shepherd, was no longer a pupil at the school and asserted without any evidence that no pupils or members of staff were on the premises at the time of the killing. He himself wasn't there so he cannot know 'of his own knowledge' as the jargon is. It is just surmise, not even hearsay."

"You knew him?" I asked

"He was the head from Hell!" Micah still had a tinge of bitterness from her three decades of teaching. "He was parachuted into the school when it was privatised, at a vastly increased salary of course."

"What is his subject?" I asked.

"Being a pain in the behind," Micah said. It was clear I wasn't going to find out much more about Mr Lawson until she was ready.

The Shepherds lived in High Salvington, a stone's throw from the John Selden if it weren't for the houses in between.

"Mr Shepherd, Mrs Shepherd, we would like to offer our condolences on the tragic death of your son, Karl."

"Well I can't see as how your condiments are going to do us any good," Mr Shepherd growled.

"Now then, Alix, don't go jumping down their throats. I'm sure they mean well.

Alix obliged with a mumble that might have been an apology.

"I understand your feelings, Mr Shepherd. It is a shocking case. Do the police have any leads?"

The stream of colourful invective from Mr Shepherd might be loosely translated as "no."

"What was young Karl like?" asked Micah.

"Well he wouldn't thank you for the 'young Karl' lark, Mrs McLairy, I can tell you that for nothing. Don't you remember me?"

"Alix Shepherd. Weren't you a pupil of mine once upon a time?"

"Once upon a time is right. I didn't hold much with school and school didn't hold much with me. That Lawson now. When I found he was to become head of Karl's school I honestly thought about taking him away didn't I, Claire? Yes, I should've too seeing as what's happened now."

"You don't blame Mr Lawson for the murder?" Micah asked innocently. I could tell that she would have been only too pleased if Alix had answered, "Yes I do."

"Not directly no but I know he poisoned the staff against Karl. Didn't I say so, Claire? Didn't I tell you that Mrs Gren was picking on the lad and turning the other kids against him? Didn't I say that?"

It seemed that Mrs Shepherd didn't have to say anything to confirm Mr Shepherd's statments. He always knew he was right anyway. Micah took her aside to ask to see Karl's room. It took the two of them away from Mr Shepherd which proved to be very useful. She looked at me on her return to indicate it was a worthwhile discussion and I cut short giving Mr Shepherd a good listening to.

He was of the 'spare the rod and spoil the child' school of parenting. It was apparent Karl had reached an age at which he would have no more of it and I got the distinct impression that he was frightened that his son might take retaliation for years of abuse.

"I'll tell you all about my chat with Claire later. For now, we have an appointment with Der Fuhrer."

Micah smiled. "The Biology teacher? It's a joke, Craig. MRS GREN is an acronym for the characteristics of living organisms - Movement, Respiration, Sensitivity, Growth, Reproduction, Excretion and Nutrition. Didn't they teach you anything in Biology? We will get a list of everyone who taught Karl in the later years in school. I think it will be possible to get that information from Lawson. We will take Barker with us."

"Because..."

"Lawson is terrified of dogs, including old softies like Barker."

"Mr McLairy, Mrs McLairy, I understand you are private investigators. I would like to know why I should be talking to you and not to the police."

Lawson's office seemed to be a sanctuary to keep him away from the pupils and probably the staff as well. He was ably defended by a secretary, Mrs Shelley who immediately took charge of Barker and tempted him away from der Fuhrer by offering him dog treats. She clearly knew her boss well.

"I think, Mr Lawson, that the police are governed by rules and duty bound to disclose information. We assure discretion and I am sure that would be in the best interests of the school," I said.

Lawson nodded at that but continued, "The school is not involved in this event at all."

"Of course, headmaster, but the murder did take place on the premises and young Shepherd had climbed a spiked fence to get to the courtyard so he might have been meeting someone here. In fact he must have met somebody because the wound was not self-inflicted."

Lawson grabbed at the word, "Self-inflicted, you say. Is it possible?"

"Sadly not. There were two stab wounds and one of them was post-mortem so unlikely to have been inflicted by the victim."

"Unlikely but not impossible?"

"Sadly impossible, headmaster. I expressed myself badly."

"I hope you will be more precise in future. I can rely on your statement that you will be discrete, I hope."

"Absolutely. We would like any information you have about which teachers Shepherd was likely to know from his time here and any pupils he was particularly friendly with."

"'With whom he was particularly friendly,' I think you mean. Mrs Shelley will provide you with any information of that nature on your way out. I have a lot of data statements to compile you know."

He gestured to his empty desk to show how hard-pressed he was.

The list of sixth form teachers was:

Mr Bailey - Maths

Mr Old and Mr Tirier - Physics

Ms Lloyd (not Mrs Gren) - Biology

As for friends, she wasn't aware of any friends but thought it wasn't her job to keep track of who was friendly with whom.

We arranged an interview with Mr Bailey in the afternoon, taking up one of his valuable free periods.

As a final request, Micah asked who ran the cadet force in the school. It was a Mr Bull, known, Mrs Shelley thought, to the pupils as "Aberdeen Angus".

As we adjourned for lunch, Micah was able to tell me about Karl Shepherd's room.

"There was a photo taken in the cockpit of an Airbus. The autopilot was in control but the photo made it look as though he was flying. Claire said that he was always going on about flying a plane into a tall building and how much damage it could cause. She was convinced that was just to wind his father up."

"Karl never took revenge for Alix's 'tough love' as Claire thought of it. What he did do was to tell him tall tales. The Mrs Gren story was one. Then, every time he got a small parcel in the post he would say, 'the poison has arrived' and look at Alix. When he went to the cadets, and he went every week, he would come back and tell Alix how easily he could shoot him from half a mile away with the aid of a telescopic sight and a Kalashnikov.

"It was all in fun, Claire thought."

"A strange idea of fun that young man had," I said.

Micah nodded.

Mr Bailey, Colin to his friends, was in his mid-forties and wore an aged tweed jacket. Like all mathematicians he was pathologically lazy. The slow manner of his probably prompted the pupils to give him the scarcely novel soubriquet of "Old Bailey".

We talked for a while about the joy of quadratic equations before getting on to the topic of his former pupil.

"Shepherd (all pupils were referred to by surname) was in the top fifty percentile of his year group and occasionally his work strayed into the top forty percentile. Then it would stray back again as soon as he got on to anything involving calculus. Unfortunately in Further Maths, practically everything does involve calculus."

"He had something of an obsession with death. He did a statistics project on the Hiroshima bomb. Apart from the macabre subject matter it was one of his better pieces of work. He was in the cadets. I know the rest of the country has Air Cadets and Army Cadets, we have stuck with a Combined Cadet Force here under the inestimable Major Bull. I advise you to call him Major by the way, he gets very shirty when the name Aberdeen Angus is mentioned. It is mentioned by a member of staff practically every day so he is a little tetchy most of the time."

"The people who can tell you most about Shepherd are his friends. Only one springs to mind and that is Dartmouth, not the poky old town you understand but a boy. Alistair is his first name. In fact if you see him you can tell him his absence has been noted and there will be some extra homework coming his way. Here, I have written his details down for you."

He handed a sheet of paper to Micah.

"One last thing, Mr Bailey..."

"You want to know my whereabouts on the night before last between the hours of ten and ten thirty?"

I nodded.

"I was at home, alone. I was watching Midsomer Murders if that helps but I have no alibi. Still," he smiled, "nothing so suspicious as a watertight alibi, eh Mr McLairy?"

We had appointments with the Science teachers the following day so we took the opportunity to seek out Alistair Dartmouth.

"Have you found the little bastard?" was the greeting from Mrs Dartmouth.

"You mean..."

"I mean have you found my drunken swine of a son? He was boozing all weekend and hasn't had the brass neck to show his face around here since."

"It's Wednesday."

"I know it's bloody Wednesday. If all you've come for is to tell me what day of the week it is then you are wasting my time and yours."

"Actually we are looking into the murder of Karl Shepherd. I thought Alistair was a friend of his."

"Well he was once upon a time but they had a big bust-up. I think it was last week. Of course Alistair wouldn't tell me what it was all about but he hinted that Karl was going to come to a bad end."

"Not that he done him in," she added hastily, "He didn't have no knife see so you needn't go jumping to conclusions. He was a bad lot, that Karl. Good riddance to bad rubbish is what we used to say."

"I've no sympathy," she added unnecessarily.

As we were leaving, she took me aside and whispered, "I know this will look bad but I got the idea that Karl Shepherd was planning 'something big'. I don't know what but given his nasty streak it was probably something diabolical. So whoever did do the little swine in was doing the world a favour. It wasn't Alistair. Anyway Alistair was too Lilian Gished to stab anybody if you catch my drift."

I got the impression she was whispering to keep the information from anyone else in the house. After all I told Micah the gist of it straight away.

On, then, to Mr Tirier. Mr Old was his senior and had given the fag of seeing us to him, by pulling rank.

"Shepherd was a good girl most of the time but girls are not really suited to science you know so her marks weren't all that good." He smiled at us. The smile became a little uncertain.

"Of course, no. Forget everything I said. I meant Mary Lamb. She was completely useless. Now who was it you wanted to see me about? I really am very busy."

"To say you are really busy and a teacher is something of a tautology don't you think. I used to be a teacher," Micah put on a sympathetic tone when she needed to.

"And what's a fecking tautology when it's at home?"

"I mean being overworked is an unfortunate concomitant of teaching. Everybody is too busy to draw breath, don't you think?"

"Well not bloody English teachers. 'Concomitant' indeed. I have a lot of work to do myself."

Micah was a former English Teacher. This was not going to go well.

"So can you tell us anything about Shepherd?"

"Well no. I don't remember him at all to be honest. It was all a long time ago you know. Look, if I think of anything I'll give you a bell. Now I really must get on."

He practically pushed us out of the room.

Gwen Lloyd was more helpful.

"Ah yes, the taxi driver's boy. I always thought he had a difficult home life, Mrs McLairy. I remember you of course, you taught me English. So I don't mind telling you that I thought that child was disturbed. He had an excessive interest in alkaloids and their effects. His mother was always telling him to eat his greens. His father was quick to chastise him if he didn't so he was delighted to learn that overdosing on greens could be fatal."

"Then he read the story of the Neasden poisoner and he talked about it endlessly. For him, Graham Young wasn't a sad individual or a monster, he was something more akin to a hero. The other pupils used to rib him about it but some of them were rather frightened of him."

"His biology coursework was very impressive but he did only moderately well at the exams. It seemed he was obsessed with something else at the time and distracted from his studies. It was a pity."

"He was friendly with Alistair Dartmouth I think but Alistair didn't go on to do Biology to A level, more's the pity."

"Anyway, Mrs McLairy,"

"Do call me Micah."

"Micah? Like the prophet? Really? Well anyway, Micah, I hope you catch the killer. Karl Shepherd was an odd fish but nobody deserves death."

As we went home, Micah was unusually quiet. This normally meant she was thinking and it was a good idea for me to remain silent. Eventually she spoke.

"There are two possibilities. I don't like either of them."

When we got home, she made a late night phone call to Mrs Shepherd and asked her three questions.

"Did Karl ever rib his father about his failing eyesight?"

"How did you...sorry. Look I won't say anything too loud you know but yes he did. He used to play tricks on Alix."

"Would you say Alix had an excessive deference for authority?"

"Well, for crying out loud, he was in the army. It was bred into him, so to speak."

The last question seemed more random.

"Did Karl own a gun?"

"Of course not. Only an old air pistol but that hardly counts."

After those three questions, Micah insisted on driving back to make a late-night call to Major Bull. My attempt to phone him from the car was fruitless. However, eventually his phone was picked up.

"Hello. Who is this?" It was a female voice, possibly Mrs Aberdeen Angus.

"Craig McLairy. We are investigating..."

"I know all about that. Come quickly. Don't waste any more time. Just get here!"

Micah checked that she had the old taser she picked up on the internet for fifty dollars with her and put her foot down.

Micah can drive like a maniac at times. This does not unduly upset me. I just close my eyes and go to sleep.

Despite the lateness of the hour, every light in the Bull residence was blazing into the night and Mrs Bull was standing in the doorway ready for us. Her face was a picture of distress.

"How can we help?" I asked.

She gestured wordlessly to invite us inside. I went in. Micah had concealed the taser about her person and she followed me in.

What we found was the large body of the late Major sprawled on the sitting-room carpet.

I said quietly to Micah, "Even old Winter can't call this a heart attack."

There was a tiny red tail from a dart protruding from the neck.

Micah checked Mrs Bull was out of earshot before saying,"This didn't cause his death on its own, it must have been tipped with poison."

To Mrs Bull, she said, "Have you called an ambulance."

"Can't you see he's dead?"

"Have you called the police?"

"I thought you should see him first. I'll call them now."

She looked at Major Bull's corpse one last time before calling. "He gave his life to that school," she said. Then she realised what she had just said and started sobbing. Micah called the cops.

"This must sound pointless, Mrs Bull. Have there been any outbreaks of illness at the school that you know of?"

"This doesn't look like an illness to me. I always told him, 'those who live by the gun will die by the gun' and I wish to God I hadn't been proved right."

"Gun?" I asked.

"That is a .177 air pistol dart. It was probably tipped with an alkaloid poison, my guess would be tubocurarine – the nasty ingredient in curare. There are literally ten thousand places you can get it on the internet and it is as deadly as," Micah gestured towards the Major.

"So there hasn't been an outbreak of sickness at school?"

"I don't know what you are on about, Mr McLairy, but no there hasn't."

We waited for the police to arrive and made Mrs Bull a cup of tea. She then indicated she would prefer a glass of the Major's whisky. She was on the verge of drinking a pint of it before Micah suggested it would probably be better somewhat diluted.

We were not drinking.

As soon as we could reasonably absent ourselves (in fact the police preferred us out of the way) we went off.

"To the school?" I asked.

"We need to find the right place."

"The right place" proved to be a clump of trees with a reasonable view of the Courtyard of Shadows. Fortunately the moon was shining brightly. Unfortunately it started to drizzle.

As we waited, Micah whispered an explanation of her questions to Mrs Shepherd.

"Claire Shepherd is one of those rare people who always tell the exact truth but invariably misconstrue the information they have. Alix's poor eyesight could lead to him losing his job as a taxi driver. He refuses to acknowledge he has any problem seeing. We already know the result of that. I think.

"The police had identifying paperwork from the body in the courtyard. They said it was Karl Shepherd. Alix couldn't rely on the evidence of his own eyes and he was used to obeying orders. He wrongly identified the body. The police would have found out in the end. The DNA and dental records would be all wrong. By that time it might have been too late. It still might, you realise."

"So it was Alistair's body all along?"

Micah nodded.

"He turned up to stop Karl from carrying out his plan."

"He succeeded that night but there is no reason why Karl shouldn't try again tonight."

"So if we put together his fascination with poisons and the detail that this courtyard is right next to the school kitchens..."

"And the food for today is delivered in about twenty minutes from now...Shh"

I had noticed a deeper shadow moving in the darkness. We waited until the lorry arrived and moved towards the courtyard behind it. Karl Shepherd was later found to be carrying two commando knives, a nunchaku and his trusty Webley air pistol. It was as well we had the element of surprise. Also there were two of us.

I put the handcuffs on him and phoned the police while Micah concealed her taser.

"The poor chap seems to have had some kind of seizure," she said.

"That's cold."

"Well it's five am and it's been raining. Also he is a murderer."

Well I couldn't argue with that.

The police had to adjust their records when it turned out reports of Karl Shepherd's death had been somewhat exaggerated. They tried unsuccessfully to charge Alix with perjury. He did lose his job though because his employers thought an eye-test was in order.

As for the resurrected Karl, Inspector Ben Tillotson reported to us on Friday in the John Selden that he was carrying enough poison to kill a regiment.

"You two have saved a lot of lives," he concluded.

"So it's your turn to buy the drinks?" I wondered.

"No I wouldn't go that far."

Death of a Cheat

We don't take matrimonial cases except when we are short of money. We are always short of money.

"My name is Strange," was the introductory gambit of the woman who approached me as Micah, Barker and I were holding a business meeting in the John Selden.

"How strange exactly?" Micah couldn't resist asking.

"Celia Strange," she replied with a long-suffering look which suggested that she had had that response before.

Micah was all business with her notebook out writing down "Celia Strange." as our new client sat down.

"It comes from the Old French 'estrange' which refers to an outsider from the area. At least that is what my husband, Martin Strange, once told me. Of course that was in the days when I believed a single word that reptile said."

"Now I know you don't take matrimonial cases but I think you will make an exception in this case."

"Why?" I asked.

"You need the money."

Such questions as 'how do you know that?' sprang to mind but I kept them to myself.

"Martin works as an accountant. It is a nine to five type of job. Now he has started coming home at about 11 one day every other week. All I want you to do is find out where he is going on those occasions to set my mind at rest."

"Just to be clear. You want to stay with this reptile if we can find out a reasonable explanation for his late nights?"

Celia nodded.

"Have you tried asking him?"

"Of course."

We waited.

"Well I didn't believe his answer. The traffic in Worthing can't make anyone six hours late every other week can it?"

Micah took down details of where the erring Martin Strange worked and the approximate dates on which he came home late. She stated our fees. Celia laughed and bargained them down by about half before the discussion was finished. She really did have a handle on our finances and I wondered why.

So it was that I found myself sitting in Micah's car outside Mr Strange's place of business on a probable straying night. We followed him discretely, or as discretely as one can when a large Alsatian is indicating in no uncertain terms that he is quite ready for dinner now.

We followed him almost to his own front door and then decided to call it a night. Barker was quite pleased at this turn of events and we considered asking a neighbour to take care of him for our next foray which was to be the following night.

We had the next day to attend to our other cases. We didn't have any other cases so we took Barker for a long, long walk. It would probably make things easier for our obliging neighbour that evening if he were not too lively.

So it was just Micah and myself tailing Strange from his respectable accountancy firm to his destination. When he parked we carried on to park in the next street. I had taken a note of the number of the house. Micah's friend Google was able to tell us it was the premises of Shangri-La Massage Parlour.

That was probably all the evidence Mrs Strange needed but I am nothing if not thorough. I decided that the Shangri-La Massage Parlour needed a visit from a fire safety officer. Micah has printed me out a number of credentials. One of them is from West Sussex County Council and authorises me to inspect premises to see they are in compliance with fire regulations. Since the cuts, there has been nobody to do this job so it was unlikely the joint had had a previous visit in five years.

I made an amicable arrangement with the madam, who gave her name as Lotus Blossom. I suspect this was not her real name but that didn't concern me. I gave her five minutes to usher her clients out of the premises while I had a cup of tea out of their view.

I can't recommend the tea but I expect people came to the Shangri-La Massage Parlour for something else. Micah was surreptitiously photographing the clients as they left. A text message from her told me that Strange was not among them. He must still have been on the premises.

I had to give the premises a good going over. Ms Blossom couldn't remember when the staff last had a fire drill and I noted this down on an official-looking form.

"And do you have a fire extinguisher?"

"A what?"

"A fire extinguisher."

"Well, we don't have no fire."

"The premises will still need one and I expect to see one next time. I need to go over the premises to see about the fire exits but I won't take long. Thank you for the tea."

And so it was that I came across Strange in a room on his own. He had a computer, a book of up-to-date tax regulations and the usual paraphernalia of an accountant. We chatted about fire regulations for a while and he promised to put Kitty, that was one of "Lotus Blossom's" other names, on the right track.

In the car back home, I told Micah, "The only ones he was cheating on were possibly his employer and the Inland Revenue. He was paid in cash for his work. Cheating on the tax man is par for the course for an accountant."

"Mrs Strange will be very pleased with this," I concluded.

"Or hopping mad, depending on what she really wanted," Micah said.

"They are both book-keepers," she added. I never ask where Micah gets her information anymore. So much information is there for the taking on the internet that she hardly needs to employ her dark arts to get hold of it.

"She works for the local bank. Of course, our accounts are confidential but she couldn't resist letting on that she knew we were in dire straits financially. Make sure you get every penny of our fee from her tomorrow."

Barker was so pleased to see us, it was as if we had deserted him for months.

"Mrs Strange, I have the information you required."

"So you caught the cheating rat with his pants down."

"We have completed the job and here is a list of our incidental expenses. You will find it quite reasonable," Micah said.

"We accept cash, cheque or visa card payments," I added.

"I will only pay if you've got the dirt on that swine."

"We have done the job you asked us to do and we can give you all the information you asked for," I said.

"But not before you get your money, I see."

She wrote out a cheque with extreme reluctance and we told her all we knew about the Shangri-La Massage Parlour.

"And you're quite sure there wasn't any monkey business on the side?"

"He seemed absorbed in his book-keeping calculations and he was paid cash in hand. He wouldn't accept payment in services."

"So I could go to his bosses about his moonlighting activities or to the Inland Revenue about his tax evasion?"

"That's up to you of course. You might think you need his income to supplement your earnings from the Nationwide Building Society and it would be hard if he lost his job."

"How did you know..."

"Who you work for? Well, we are a detective agency, Mrs Strange. Now if we have no further business here, we have a hungry dog waiting for us."

"Do you think our client was reassured that her husband wasn't playing away with Kitty and her gang?" Micah asked on the way home.

"Quite the reverse, I think. Do people really want to find their erring partners are not playing away? Or do they come to us expecting the worst and being disappointed when we don't find it?"

"Very philosophical. It's your turn to cook tonight."

We had an Irish stew with every vegetable under the sun mixed with oxtail soup, potatoes and sausages. It tastes every bit as good as it sounds.

For the next six months, we were able to concentrate on a number of mind-numbingly boring but rather lucrative cases. I didn't think of Mrs Strange much but I had an occasional vision of her tracking our bank account. I imagined sometimes she was pleased we were doing well but then she didn't realise how brain-dead the cases made us feel. She little realised that she was going to provide us with our first murder case for far too long. If she had she would have been less than pleased.

On More Radio, we heard the following. "Police are baffled (I always prick up my ears when I hear that expression. I also switch on my phone to record the story for Micah) by the horrific murder of a middle-aged woman in a deserted property in central Worthing. The body was discovered by a rough sleeper who was aiming to spend the night at the property but thought better of the idea when he discovered the space was already occupied by a corpse. The body has been identified by dental records as that of a Mrs Celia Strange."

"Her husband, Mr Martin Strange of Moneysaver Accountancy Services, is helping the police with their inquiries."

One section of the internet which is not wide open to Google is the police service. That does not mean that it is closed to Micah however. She suspects that old Ben Tillotson has actually made her access easier but then she does help the police with their inquiries herself from time to time.

When she brought Barker back from his walk, I played back the radio broadcast to her.

She nodded, "I know, I listened to it on my phone."

In response to my unasked query, she added, "The police computer system hasn't got any information as yet. I will give them another hour."

I made some sardine sandwiches and we shared them as she sought to find out what the boys in blue had been able to ascertain. After a while, she said, in an attempt to put me off my sandwich perhaps,

"The body was the subject of a frantic attack. We already knew that the face had been cut up because the police had to rely on dental records to identify the corpse. It had been dismembered and wrapped in a plastic sheet. The body was not complete. The right hand was missing. The subject's car had been caught on CCTV in Broadwater at ten thirty PM the previous night.

"After a while, they were able to get an alibi out of Strange."

"Let me guess, the Shangri-La Massage Parlour."

"Yes, but Miss Kitty couldn't alibi him for the possible time of the murder so the police are holding him pending further inquiries. I think it is time for that follow-up fire safety visit, don't you?"

I nodded.

Kitty had not installed a fire extinguisher. Indeed she was not entirely clear on what one was. I showed her on Google and then showed her how to order online. She looked at me as if I were demonstrating some kind of black magic.

In the interim, we chatted. She would not talk about clients but she was quite happy to talk about her book-keeper. This itself seemed to confirm my previous thoughts about Mr Strange not being up to any hanky-panky except in relation to the Inland Revenue. Whether he murdered his wife was another matter.

"He didn't talk much about his wife. In fact, he didn't talk much at all except about VAT receipts and that financial doolally just went right over my head as you might imagine." I imagined that Kitty was nowhere near as dumb as she made out. To run this business must have taken more intelligence than she gave herself credit for.

"He did say, or suggest at least, that Celia was having an affair but he hadn't pursued it because he didn't really want to find out if you know what I mean."

I reported this snippet of information to Micah. Micah had a lot of information of her own. It seemed that Inspector Ben Tillotson had obligingly uploaded the post-mortem results, the interview with Mr Strange and a report from WPC Swift to his laptop which was unsecured. He could get the sack for that but we rather hoped he didn't.

"The mutilation was post-mortem."

Micah let that sink in.

I said, "the killer was trying to conceal the identity but was disturbed – otherwise why did they cut off only one hand? They reckoned without the dental records."

Micah added, "And the DNA. Mrs Strange's DNA was on file from a previous unrelated investigation and that matched too. She choked on a condom. No DNA was retrievable from it."

"Mr Strange's interview," she continued, "indicated that he went home after doing the books at the Shangri-La Massage Parlour. The police, incidentally, have reported his untaxed work to the Inland Revenue but they think that is all they can get him on. He said that he was home alone without any witnesses but he is lucky enough to have a nosy neighbour who can recall him coming home at ten. He could not easily have got to the murder site from his home without his car. The neighbour did not hear the car in the night and is one of those people who notice everything."

"Mr Strange was not surprised that Celia was not home because she had taken to spending the night with her aunt Hilda who was quite unwell and living in warden-controlled accommodation in Croydon."

"WPC Swift was a bit rambling in her verbatim report but it is quite interesting. It seems that Hilda Bush's flat was 'as clean as a new pin' and Mrs Hilda Bush herself was described as 'sprightly'. She offered tea, put the kettle on and promptly forgot about it. She answered 'Yes' to every question. Yes, Mrs Strange was often there overnight. Was she there on the night of the fifteenth? Yes. That was the night she was killed.

"You don't choke on a condom visiting your sick aunt," I said quite unnecessarily. Micah gave me a look and continued.

"The report continues, if you can avoid interrupting,

'I asked if Mrs Strange had stayed overnight on the sofa.'

'"I suppose so," was the answer.'

'You suppose so?'

'That's what I said, young lady. Now shall I make you some tea?'

Mrs Bush put the kettle on and complained about the price of sugar.

'A shilling a pound if you can believe it. I've written to Queen Margaret about it.'

'Queen Margaret?'

'Margaret Thatcher as was. She is still on the throne I hope, young lady.'

'I assured her that Margaret Thatcher was still on the throne and left without any tea. Mrs Bush had forgotten about it again. I concluded that no useful evidence could be gathered from this witness.'

"You know," said Micah conversationally, "the NHS is still using an outdated Windows system which has more holes in it than a colander. Mrs Bush's medical records might as well have been posted on Facebook."

She brought up the appropriate page and we both looked at it. Hilda Bush suffered from many of the illnesses associated with old age but she had been specifically tested for memory loss. She was not likely to think Margaret Thatcher was on the throne, although reputedly Margaret Thatcher herself had that delusion.

'And look at the address," I said.

Mr Strange had given the right block of flats but the number was out by one digit.

We divided our resources. Micah went to the seafront. She works for a charity which delivers food to the homeless people who are to be found in the shelters along Worthing seafront and she thought she might usefully inquire after the witness who had found the body. It was likely to be a subject of some gossip.

I headed for Green Lane in Croydon.

Mrs Bush's flat was as clean as a badly-maintained council tip. I asked her about the police visit. Apparently, her neighbour, Tilly, had told her all about it but omitted the detail of what they were asking her about. She was most upset the young lady wouldn't have any tea because Tilly hadn't got any sugar.

Mrs Bush offered me some tea. It was surprisingly good despite the state of the cup which was last cleaned in the days of Queen Margaret.

"Did your niece, Celia, stay with you on the fifteenth?"

"Are you a friend of that reptile?"

I thought this was a reference to Mr Strange and assured her I wasn't.

"Well then yes, no, wait a minute. I think we both know that was the night she was strangled to death so no she certainly wasn't here."

"Strangled to death?"

"Strangled. Actually, the radio said choked but that comes to the same thing. It was a terrible waste."

"And she often came to stay with you?"

There was a pause.

"No young man. Now she has gone to a better place I don't think it matters so much. The truth of the matter was that we used to Skype and WhatsApp once in a while and she was always sure to tell me that if the reptile were to ask I was to say she had spent the night with me. I think she just went for a girls' night out myself, don't you?"

I made a noise which might have meant yes, or no.

"Now how about a cup of tea, unless you fancy a drop of scotch?"

"I'm driving," I said.

"I don't mind telling you that my Fred didn't hold with those drink driving laws," she said as she put on the kettle, "mind you it was the death of him in the end. The drink that is, not the driving."

The rest of the afternoon was spent reminiscing about the good old days when you could drive when you were as p*ssed as a newt. We talked about her late husband, who did just that until the cirrhosis caught up with him.

Meanwhile, Micah had been talking to a man called Jock. He had no surname – none that he would share anyway – and the forename was because of the original reason that he was from Scotland.

"It was pissing it down, begging your pardon, it was raining a lot. God it was raining. I haven't seen rain like that since Noah put all those animals on the Ark. That was a joke by the way. Please yourself obviously."

There was then a rambling discussion about how thirsty Jock was. He turned down Micah's offer of water because he knew what fish did in that stuff. That was a joke too apparently. Micah's charity, Worthing Churches Homeless Project, has strict rules about buying alcohol for alcoholics and Micah stuck to them although that meant it took longer to get his story out of our Jock.

"It was a church. It used to be a church anyhow but it was desegregated (Micah was under no obligation to correct his vocabulary and didn't want to interrupt the flow now there was one) and nobody had bought the property as yet. It was dry, you see."

"Was it locked?"

"Not seriously, no. I don't think little Lord Jesus wanted me freezing to death in the rain now did he? Anyway it wasn't me that bust the lock. That was done about a week before by some dosser or other. When I got in there, there was no light. Now I remember clearly, I heard someone leaving but I thought nothing of it. I think I'd be a bit clearer with a can of Tennants."

I imagine Micah shook her head at this point.

"Well have it your own way. Jesus drank wine you know. Anyway I wasn't concerned if anyone chose to go out in the rain. The light in the old church was bad. It was only when a car went by that the headlights showed up the body. It was like something out of Dennis Wheatley. You know, a human sacrifice. I'm sorry to say I threw up in the church. I know you're not supposed to do that but these weren't normal circumstances. The body, I could tell it was a woman, but it was really badly cut up. That's all I remember.

"Before you go, do you want me to tell you a joke?"

Micah did. It was diabolical.

"So Jock almost saw the murderer. Someone with blood all over them going out into the street. There weren't too many people around in the rain and the bloodstains could go under a raincoat until they got home. We are no nearer to knowing who it was though."

"Any ideas, Craig?"

"You said the Stranges were gifted with a nosy neighbour."

"Mrs Delia Roach of number 17, yes. I think we might pay her a visit to find out what she knows. If she kept an eye on Mr Strange she must have seen a lot about Mrs Strange as well. We'll take Barker. He is a great ice-breaker."

"Unless Delia hates dogs," I said.

"Accentuate the positive," Micah replied.

I drove to Delia's so that Micah could update Inspector Tillotson by email on her interview with Jock.

"Hello, you're a Labrador aren't you?"

Barker didn't enlighten her so I didn't either.

"Mrs Roach..."

"Oh call me Delia, please, Mr McLairy. And I shall call you Craig and Micah."

She observed our confusion with amusement and added, "I am a bit of a detective myself, Craig. I must warn you I know everything. And you did have your old photos on that ad you had in the *Worthing Herald* you know. Those photos must have been about ten years old at a guess but I recognised you anyway. 'No job too small. Absolute discretion guaranteed.' I believe."

We had had no response from the adverts so I had assumed nobody had read them. Apparently, Delia had at least seen them which was gratifying in its way although it hadn't repaid the cost of the adverts.

"And I can tell a Labrador from an Alsatian," she added.

"We are inquiring..."

"...about the Strange family over the road. Come on, Micah, we both know there has been a murder and that is your forte. 'No job too small' was misleading advertising. I can tell you something quite interesting about Mrs Strange."

She paused. She looked at our expressions and laughed.

"No. I don't want any payment. I just want the villain caught. Or do you call him 'chummy'? Anyway, I can tell you about Mrs Strange's little 'chummy'. A car has called over the road. It has always been when Mr Strange was about his business or one of his businesses. I understand a bit of monkey business at a massage parlour was his hobby. The registration number..."

She gave us the number.

"It was a white Astra. Quite an ordinary car but I have seen it somewhere else too and a friend of mine works in the shop it was parked outside. I casually asked and they casually told me. It belongs to a Mr Chase who buys his sausages there. He likes his sausages. And he likes to be called 'Al'. And I'll tell you another thing. My friend at the butcher's is about my age and I don't have any illusions. That didn't stop 'call me Al' from trying to chat her up. I think that tells you something."

"Tell me, Micah, are you familiar with the word 'gigolo'?"

Micah smiled.

"Well, I think we understand each other. He is a good twenty years younger than Mrs Strange. I don't know if he killed her but you have to start looking somewhere. I alibied Mr Strange for the time of the murder and you can take my word that it wasn't him. I know it is usually the husband."

At this point, she looked at me and I don't find that amusing.

"Who's driving?"

Micah owned up.

"Well have a glass of Merlot with me, Craig. I am sure you are not the murdering kind."

With the name and the car number, it was a matter of moments for Micah to find out where 'call me Al' lived. That was our next port of call. Micah dutifully updated old Ben Tillotson with the information.

"It is as well to tell the police where we are going if this man really is a murderer," she said.

...

"Can we talk to Mr Chase?"

"Hardly. He's been dead these ten years."

"Mr Al Chase."

"Oh dear. Is he in trouble again?" The woman we took to be his mother looked at me and then at Micah appraisingly.

"You know that boy has had a hundred jobs since his father went to a better place but his hobby has always been chasing the ladies, bless him. It gets him in loads of scrapes I can tell you."

"Where might we find him?" I asked.

"Are you an angry husband?" she asked.

"Not as a rule," Micah said quietly,

Mrs Chase considered for a moment and then said, "he'll be down the Black Sheep. If you are an angry husband you can give him a clip round the ear from me, the little scamp."

I found the 'little scamp' at the bar of the Black Sheep. I had decided not to take Micah with me but I did follow her advice and recorded the conversation.

We are Englishmen so when we met we talked about the weather. He let me buy him a drink. Then he let me buy him another. He seemed to have left his wallet at home. I suspect he often left his wallet at home.

By the third drink, I was his 'bes' mate. Bes' mate in the whole wassisname. I steered the conversation towards the tragic death of Mr Strange. It was still a topic of gossip.

He told me that we were both men of the world. He told me several times. Looking around the bar, he confided to me that he had known the lady. He had known her very well if I understood what he meant.

"Very well indeed," he emphasised.

"Then the Jezebel went and dumped me. Here do you want another drink?"

He had forgotten that he had forgotten his wallet and bought me a drink. The barman thought this was an unprecedented event, judging by his expression.

"Yes. Dumped me. Me! And do you know what? Do you you know what? She wanted to go off with someone more interesting. She'd been seeing him for weeks, so she said."

At this point, his drinking companions decided that if he was flashing the cash for once it would be worth joining in the conversation. They were full of the shortcomings of Mrs Strange and one comment, in particular, struck Micah and myself as significant.

"Poor Al, he was quite cut up about it. I remember last Wednesday he was in here and let's just say he was in a bit of a state. He stayed till closing time drowning his sorrows, didn't you, Al?"

Al concurred and got his friend to buy him another drink. His wallet had gone home again apparently.

Micah wanted to know if this looked like a set-up alibi. It did but I had managed to get the barman to confirm it and several people had rushed to do so. Even if it was a fake it would have stood up in court.

It was some three months before we stumbled across the "somebody more interesting" who had taken Mrs Strange's fancy. I would like to say it was good solid detective work but it was more by way of a coincidence.

Micah came in from a sandwich run to the homeless people who occupy the beach front shelters in Worthing. She had come across Jock. She noticed that his arm was in a sling.

"What happened to your arm?"

"It's in a bit of pain. I think a can of Tennants would probably ease it. What do you think?"

"How did it happen?"

"The bastard had a bloody knife. Excuse my French but it was bloody after the bastard stuck it in my bloody arm. He was after something more vital but my arm got in the way."

"Who was it?"

"Well you're the detective. Go and detect that."

"You don't know who it was?"

"Man don't be daffy. Of course I know who it was but it's five years inside for carrying a knife and he might take exception to me calling the cops on him."

"Telling me isn't calling the cops."

"It'll cost you a Pavarotti. That's a tenner to you. It's a joke."

"How about a sandwich."

"That's one expensive sandwich. OK go on hand it over."

"What was his name?"

"Mmmm Mgage." said Jock with a mouthful of sandwich.

"Sorry?"

"Will Armitage. And it's no good asking his address because he hasn't got one. Like me, see."

"Thanks, Jock."

"I've got a new joke for you."

I didn't know about the accuracy of Jock as a witness but the joke was definitely not new. I remembered it from the 1950s.

Homeless people are reluctant to tell you where they are sleeping. This might be to prevent anyone else from taking over. Anywhere out of the weather is advantageous. However, Jock had made it known to Micah that he was too spooked to go back to the church where he had found the mutilated corpse.

That night found us lurking with intent in the vicinity of the building in question. Nothing. So did the next night.

To cut a long story short it was a fortnight before our surveillance paid off. And it was a rainy fortnight at that.

Micah was working on her taser which she thought had been damaged by the rain. She resorted to Google to find a manual on how to repair the thing. She was reluctant to try the disused church again and my remarks on the lines of 'once more into the breach' didn't seem to be helping.

In the end, her professionalism and, dare I say it, nosiness, pulled her out into the cold night. The west wind was enough to take the flesh off your bones. In short, it was a standard night for Worthing. The street-lighting was in poor repair and we didn't dare to use torches in case our prey was frightened away.

"At the very least he could get five years for just carrying a knife," I said encouragingly. Micah sniffled and suggested she was probably getting a cold.

"Shh."

"Don't you shh me," she began. She was not in the best of moods. I pointed to two shadows making their way to the back door of the church. We caught a stifled giggle. I looked at my watch.

"Give them five minutes," Micah was suddenly businesslike.

The luminous dial of my watch was having a job getting through the time when we were interrupted by a blood-curdling scream. It was coming from the Church.

For a couple of old-timers, we ran convincingly. Micah was busy on her phone. I wondered who she could be texting.

Through the door. Into the church. We used torches then and the scene they illuminated was not a pretty one. A man and woman were before the altar. The man was trying to force his attentions on the woman with a vicious-looking knife.

"Don't make any trouble, Candy, or you'll be feeling this."

"I think this date is going wrong," Micah said.

The man turned around and practically walked into Micah's taser. He dropped the knife and for a moment I thought we had killed him. We hadn't.

A police siren announced who Micah had been in touch with. Candy panicked.

"Look. My mum is going to kill me. I can't be seen here. You've got to let me go."

"You can go or stay. Just as you like. Only you are not the first woman to get on the wrong side of this man. You could be the last if you give evidence. I'll have a word with your mum."

Candy didn't look as if she thought Micah was going to persuade her mum out of a chance for a first-class nag but her disgust with her date overcame that. She waited for the police with us.

Old Ben Tillotson was not on duty that night so we had to spend hours telling our version of events. Micah's taser wasn't mentioned. She claimed she hit Will Armitage and he went down like a sack of potatoes. They couldn't put her fists in custody, not when her opponent had a knife.

The time must have seemed longer for Will Armitage who was locked in a cell that smelt as if a hundred drunks had used it as a toilet. For all I know they had.

Armitage had a string of convictions in various coastal towns. He continued to insist the death of Mrs Strange was an accident but his other crimes all added up to a hefty prison sentence.

One postscript to the story is the Strange's nosy neighbour, Delia Roach. We recommended her as a Neighbourhood Watch Co-ordinator and she took to the job like a duck to water.

The Case of the Haunted House

I do not believe in ghosts. However, I would not spend a night in an allegedly haunted house on my own. That was the reason Barker and I were sitting in an ill-lit house waiting for the ghosts to appear. I had a camera in case the ghosts were visible. I had a blunt instrument in the form of a monkey wrench in case the spirits turned out to be human after all. And of course I had Barker as back-up. I know he is as soft as rice pudding but a stranger might not know so much.

We have been given some odd cases in my time but this was odder yet.

"My name is Viktor Price," said the neatly-turned out man in his mid-fifties with a central-European accent. He said it as though it meant something. Perhaps it did to him.

"I have a house in Durrington which I am anxious to sell."

"We're not looking to move at the moment, Mr Price."

He gave a laugh I didn't like the sound of. It was on the edge of hysteria.

"No no no. I am having difficulty selling it because some stupid superstitious przygłup is going around saying it is haunted."

Micah wrote something in her notebook and let me see it.

"Viktor Price, Polish."

I looked briefly at his shoes. Micah scribbled "from Poland" in case there was any confusion.

I only heard the word "przygłup" once more and that was when Mr Price addressed it to me. It politely translates as 'nitwit' but I must tell this story in the right order.

I tried to explain that we were detectives not Ghostbusters. Mr Price said, "very amusing" in the tone of someone who has never found anything amusing in his life. He then named a fee which I decided I could go along with.

After dark any house will make noises. In a semi-detached house you can often hear the footsteps of your neighbour going up the stairs except that it sounds like someone coming up your stairs, possibly armed with an axe. Floorboards creak when there is nobody treading on them. The wind can sound like cries. The mind can play tricks.

The hackles on a dog really do rise when they get spooked. In the dead of night that is what happened to Barker. He moved in close to me and I think he would have liked to get inside my jacket. There was definitely something he did not want to see.

I got up reluctantly and persuaded Barker that we were going on a ghost hunt. Since the only way he could stay with me was if he came along, he came along.

We went from room to room. Each one I came to seemed to be ghost-free. I was gaining in confidence by the time I got to the kitchen. Somehow my confidence drained away when I saw the staring eyes of the corpse on the floor.

I stood in the doorway and restrained Barker. Now he was no longer spooked and wanted to go and examine the corpse. I thought the police might disapprove. I recorded the following for Micah who was away on a hen-do in Manchester.

"The kitchen is large and old-fashioned. There are crystals scattered on the floor which I take to be sugar. There is a sheet on the floor and it is covered in blood. The body is that of a white female in her twenties. Her hair colour is dark and she seems to be of average height. It is difficult to determine anything about her dress as it has been slashed with a knife. None of the cuts to the dress drew blood though. The blood came from one fatal stab wound to the neck."

I could not get a signal in the kitchen so I had to drag Barker outside to put through a call to the police. They warned me in no uncertain terms not to go anywhere near the crime scene and informed me that a squad car would be with me 'directly'.

'Directly' turned out to mean three-quarters of an hour. The police forensic team got into appropriate gear and went into the house. They came out again very quickly. One sarky sergeant asked me if I would like to point out the corpse.

I showed the way to the kitchen but body was there none. I stared stupidly at the floor.

"Have you been drinking, sir?"

"No, officer."

"Taking drugs?"

"No."

"Do you often get these hallucinatons?"

It was in vain for me to protest that the body had been there less than an hour before. When the police got onto the topic of what I was doing in the house they decided I was a deluded unreliable witness. They had a point.

My detailed search of the kitchen revealed nothing except the sugar on the floor. That was still there and in my own mind, it confirmed my story. Nobody else was likely to believe it though.

Somehow the *Worthing Herald* got hold of the story. Possibly the sarky Sergeant had given it to them. "Private Detective leads police on wild goose chase." was the headline and the story did not get more complimentary as it went on.

Micah, bless her, believed me. My verbatim account of the scene in the kitchen probably swayed her but she is inclined to trust my word anyway.

"Viktor will definitely have problems selling the house now. He won't be pleased.

"Przygłup! What with you and your disappearing corpse, the peasants in these parts will believe the place is haunted until Kingdom come. I am half-inclined not to pay you."

However, he was a refreshingly honest man and handed over the rather large fee he had discussed.

"Something isn't right," said Micah.

"You can say that again," I said.

"No I mean ..." and then she trailed off into silence.

The following week I had a visitor to my office. He gave me his business card. It seemed he was a Mr West from the Psychical Phenomena Investigators plc. I was disappointed that it wasn't a client because we could have done with one.

Mr West asked me a number of detailed questions about the "phenomenon" at the haunted house. I suggested that it wasn't a phenomenon but a murder. Somewhat to my surprise, he agreed.

"But the murder didn't take place."

There was a silence.

"In 1924 the house was owned by the Black family. Anthony Black was an up-and-coming businessman and the family employed a number of servants. In the kitchen which you visited there would have been a cook, Elsie Blunt. Her description matched the body which you saw. There was also a scullery maid called Jane Turner."

"According to Jane, Elsie Blunt came up behind her when she was washing cutlery. She started tickling her. Jane Turner was one of those people who cannot abide being tickled. It was a severe physical pain to her. She turned around and tried to fend Elsie off with her hand. Unfortunately for Elsie, her hand had a knife in it."

"The jury in the case heard medical testimony. It was one of the first cases in which a member of the working classes had been able to call a psychological expert. The consequence was that the jury found her not guilty. The judge was thunderstruck as you can imagine and made a closing remark that Jane's husband had best avoid tickling her. She never married. She died in 1968."

"What about the injuries to the body?"

"Jane claimed that she didn't know what she was doing. The jury noted that all the violence was directed to Elsie's clothes rather than to a living body. The prosecution unsuccessfully tried to prove that therefore Jane murdered Elsie but the defence dismissed that as a non-sequitur."

"So there was no murder?"

"Exactly, Mr McLairy."

Mr West stayed for a cup of tea and a chat about Psychical Phenomena. He seemed a nice chap.

That was not my opinion on the following Thursday. I was in the John Selden with Micah perusing the *Worthing Herald*. It had the story, "The Detective who Sees Ghosts." I visualised the remains of my reputation going up in flames.

I very quietly folded the newspaper and returned to my Cabernet Sauvignon.

"Something is not right," Micah said.

"Tell me some good news."

"I am not sure it is good or bad but there are two things you should know. The first is that the house is not on the market."

"I can understand Mr Price taking it off after all this."

"Except that it was never on the market in the first place. It was his late uncle's house and Mr Price undertook to sell it and distribute the proceeds to the other beneficiaries. Of course, if he can't sell it then he doesn't have to distribute anything to anybody."

"You said there were two things."

"I think you should have investigated Psychical Phenomena Investigations plc more closely."

"Or indeed at all."

"Yes. The company is registered by law of course. It has only existed for a year and the main shareholder is a Mr Viktor Price."

She couldn't resist adding, "I think you've been mis-sold PPI."

It was intriguing. We were suddenly very interested in Mr Viktor Price.

"You think he is responsible for trashing your reputation?" Micah asked.

"Don't you?" I replied.

"It looks that way. We still need to know two things. The how and the why. First we should find out as much as possible about the 'who'. Give me an hour and I will know more about Viktor than Viktor knows."

That may sound like an idle boast but I know Micah. It was, if anything, a modest underestimate.

An hour later, she repaid my confidence.

"He was one of three children. The parents stayed in Poland with the eldest daughter who now looks after them. Viktor is the second eldest and his younger sister Sylwia changed the spelling of her name to Sylvia but not the pronunciation. She is in Manchester. It is a long shot and a long drive but there are no photos of her online which is suspicious in itself these days."

"There is one other reason why Sylvia might be worth having a little chat with."

Micah paused but I am an old hand at this. She was bound to say more and she did.

"She is a member of the Casualties Union. They provide acting and reacting casualties and patients for the medical profession, the emergency services, and those who teach first aid, nursing and rescue.   Their make-up skills are second to none. Interested?"

I was. We shared the drive to Manchester. It was grey and pouring with rain when we arrived. You can more-or-less identify Manchester by that.

We discussed how to approach Sylvia. We decided that Viktor had told us she was living in Manchester and since we were visiting we hoped it was all right to call round. Then Micah decided suddenly it was important that she did this on her own.

I was forced to adjourn to one bar while Micah arranged to meet Sylvia in another. We caught up later.

Over a bottle of Black Shiraz, Micah played back the relevant parts of the conversation.

"I don't think Viktor ever mentioned you, er Micah isn't it?"

"Yes, we had a business relationship."

Apparently, the look in Sylvia's eyes was a sight to behold. What sort of 'business' she thought her brother got up to with Micah we preferred not to speculate.

"Oh ah. Yes, well. Any friend of Viktor's is welcome to buy me a drink," she laughed. The laugh rang a bit hollow.

"Look, for a laugh, why don't we send him a selfie of just the two of us."

Sylvie didn't have a chance to reject this proposal because by then Micah had already taken it. She took it with a good grace.

"I suppose you know all about Maria," said Sylvia.

Matching her tone and not letting on she didn't know Maria from Madonna, Micah sympathised, "Yes it was a shame."

"It was awful for Viktor for the two of them to break up. It was a whole month before he summoned up the courage to tell our parents about the divorce. It was a separation really, they weren't technically married. She went back to Poland but never got in touch with any of the family. We weren't close, she was always a bit 'standing-off' I think is the expression. I wasn't surprised that I heard nothing from her. Neither did poor old Vic."

"How about another drink?"

"I shouldn't really. Maybe just the one. Look I can't let you pay for all the drinks, Micah."

"I'll be around for a few days, I am sure we can meet up again if you're not too busy. Cab Sav is it?"

"OK. You twisted my arm."

Then she showed me the selfie. She was watching my face.

"Jesus wept!"

"So I understand. It's her isn't it."

"The late fictional Elsie Blunt, the tickling cook. You weren't kidding about the make-up skills. What a performance. Shall I tag along next time?"

"Of course. I didn't want you there this time because it would have given the game away to Sylvia. Seeing you tomorrow should unnerve her. I mean that in the nicest possible way."

I smiled.

Sylvia Price lost her smile when she saw me. She made a half-hearted attempt to run away but Micah took her arm in an apparently friendly gesture. Micah's friendly gestures are sometimes backed with deceptively strong muscles. Sylvia collapsed back into her seat and eyed me apprehensively.

"Have we met before?" I asked.

"It was just a joke."

"Does Viktor often play jokes?"

"Well no, but he told me this was just a joke and he wasn't someone to disagree with. He said you were someone who didn't believe in ghosts and that was all I knew. That dog of yours nearly spoiled everything. He was within an inch of licking me and I couldn't have stood that. At least I couldn't have kept the pose."

"What was the sugar all over the floor about?"

"That was my own idea. I didn't want anybody creeping up on me. The sugar would have warned me of anyone who was coming."

I changed the subject.

"What do you know about Maria?"

"She was familiar with that house. She was very friendly with Uncle Drac, that's what we used to call him, his real name was Włodzimierz, you know like Vlad the Impaler. It was a joke. That's unusual for Viktor. He really didn't like Maria's friendship with Uncle Drac. They were really very friendly if you know what I mean."

We knew what she meant.

On our way back to Durrington, I drove and Micah updated Inspector Ben Tillotson. He was still full of hilarity over my ghostbusting reputation but he was a sensible man by which I mean he listened to Micah.

Ben was able to tell us that Włodzimierz Price's death had been attributed to natural causes. It came as no surprise to either of us that Doctor Winter had made that stunning diagnosis. I honestly believe if a corpse were riddled with bullets he would have it down as a case of lead poisoning.

Our priority would be to find Maria. We would have liked to find her alive.

"Thank you for calling Durrington Detective Agency. Calls may be recorded for staff training purposes."

"What staff? You haven't got any staff."

"And if and when we get them, we will need to train them. Now, what can I do for you, Mr Price?"

"Call me Viktor."

"Certainly. Apart from calling you Viktor, what can I do for you?"

"I would like to have a conversation with you but I would prefer to do it in the street. Shall we say outside your office in twenty minutes?"

"Certainly."

Mr Price's Rover drew up to the kerb precisely twenty minutes later. He looked up the road. He looked down the road. He looked across the way to make sure nobody could hear us. This was a waste of his time because I had taken up Micah's habit of having my phone on 'record' in my pocket.

"Mr McLairy, I think you have been down to Manchester to see my sister." He essayed a smile. It was not a success.

"Yes."

"Now look, about that. I apologise for my little joke but I would like to compensate you for your trouble and the trip to Manchester with a little extra for hurt feelings."

"Mmm," I said non-committally.

"I was thinking of a thou.. shall we say two thousand..."

"Mmm"

"For each of you. Would that be acceptable?"

"I will give you a receipt."

"No need for that but I must explain. My sister, she is, how shall I say, in a delicate state of mind a lot of the time and she gets these obsessions, these wasps in her bonnet and so forth. One of the biggest wasps is my former wife, Maria."

"I thought you weren't married."

"Quite, you understand. We are both men of the world. Maria was free to come and go as she chose. She chose to go. I don't know why. I think she went back to the old country but even there I cannot be sure. I trust we understand each other."

And here his tone changed.

"You will not investigate this matter any further, Mr McLairy. You have wasted too much time already I'm sure and the good book says that the time is money is it not? So leave it out, my friend."

I have never been called 'my friend' in quite such a threatening manner before.

The four thousand pounds duly arrived. I was able to claim gift aid when I gave it to Micah's favoured charity which meant we had a record that every penny we got from Viktor had gone to a good cause.

I replayed the conversation to Micah and she forwarded the information to Inspector Ben Tillotson that evening.

"Thank you for calling Durrington Detective Agency. Calls may be recorded for staff training purposes."

"Come off it, you don't have any staff."

"Hello, Ben. Have you any good news for me?"

"Well I have heard all about the bribe you took from Mr Price. Micah says it is all going to a good cause and I'm sure it is."

If it were possible to wink over an audio phone I am sure old Ben would have done so.

"We ransacked your haunted house. Mr Price wasn't at all pleased but we said we were looking for ectoplasm. We found nothing."

There was a pause.....

"...except a letter from Maria to her uncle-in-law. I wouldn't dream of reading out any of the contents over the telephone it would contravene the Wireless Telegraphy Act. It confirms Sylvia's assertion that they were very close indeed. It was at the back of a drawer and Viktor had obviously overlooked it."

"The other thing was that one of our WPCs noticed that the concrete floor in the basement was new and according to her it had been done all wrong. It is no crime to lay a basement floor 'all wrong' but we thought it prudent to have a closer look. The x-ray showed us the skeleton of a young woman about a foot below the surface."

"It was a long job to get the body out intact but there can be no doubt that this was the body of Maria Price. Together with your evidence of the measures our Vik took to conceal the body it should be enough to get a conviction."

"Then and only then your reputation can be restored. Until then..."

And he thought it hilariously funny to play the Ghostbusters' theme for my benefit.

Death Watch

"It seems that Aaron Stephens really did die of a heart attack. That wasn't a result of the limited imagination of Dr Winter. It was the considered opinion of a pathologist who could be relied on to tie his own shoelaces." Inspector Ben Tillotson had dropped in for a pint of Harveys at the John Selden. He never 'dropped in' unless he wanted something.

I waited for him to continue.

"The first person on the scene relieved the corpse of his wallet and watch but they missed a twenty pound note in his back pocket. Aaron had a history of heart trouble and his poor old ticker just gave up. He had been on a bit of a health kick according to Mrs Stephens, eating rabbit food. It won't make you live longer. It'll just seem longer. Stephens knows that now."

"Where was the body found?" I asked. Ben noticed that Micah had her notebook and pen suitably poised.

"It was found in Exmoor Drive at 8 am. It is usually quiet around that time. The road is supposedly on the route of the number 7 bus but nobody has ever seen one there and the locals are too canny to think of queuing at either of the bus stops. The body was found by Prince, the French Bulldog owned by a Mrs Percival who was taking him for a morning stroll. She has vowed never to go that way again because she was worried about the impact on Prince's nerves."

"So as I say, it was an open and shut case."

"But you are not happy?"

"No, Craig." (the very fact old Ben called me by my first name led me to believe he wanted something from us), "I have a feeling in my bones. There is something funny. I don't mean Les Dawson funny, I mean 'brides in the bath' funny if you see what I mean."

He went on to explain to us that the 'brides in the bath' case referred to George Joseph Smith whose three brides had all perished apparently from natural causes in remarkably similar circumstances.

"The pathologist got that one wrong although it was only the coincidence that three of his brides (he was never legally married to any of them) died in the same way that aroused suspicion."

"So have there been similar deaths?"

"Possibly. A Mr Colin Spelman also died from a heart attack. He had also adopted a regime of drugs, diet and exercise following an angina attack. The drugs were the usual melange of beta blockers, statins, blood thinners and ACE inhibitors and there was no sign anyone had tampered with them and no signs of violence to the body."

"However..." I prompted.

"However, he died in his own home and his wallet and watch were never found. It was put down to sloppiness or greed on the part of the investigating team but I am not so sure."

"Both cases are closed. That is to say they are closed to me."

"They are not closed to us," I said. Micah nodded.

"I call that a good day's work. I'll let you buy me another pint of Harveys if you please."

I didn't please but I did it with a good grace.

"He finds Les Dawson funny?" was Micah's first observation when our guest had returned to his duties.

"It takes all sorts," I said, "The case seems interesting though. I take it nobody observed anything or old Ben would have said so. It would be interesting to find the light-fingered Larry who made off with the wallet and watch."

"The thief might be the murderer."

"I don't know that you can induce a heart attack to order and then rob the body."

"I can't but who knows; perhaps he or she can."

"We have decided not to put Prince on the list of suspects."

Micah gave a me a look which suggested that was a remark in very bad taste. Barker was too busy wolfing down doggie treats to notice.

"The first thing to do would be to find a connection between Spelman and Stephens."

"Apart from their initial letter."

Micah has some funny ideas at times.

"Of course there may not be one. The 'brides in the bath' murderer was connected to all his victims and stood to gain from their deaths. Other serial killers have killed more-or-less at random for the joy of killing."

"And of course we have not established that it was murder in either case, or do you trust the feeling in old Ben's bones?"

"I think we should investigate the facts and find out what we can," I suggested.

"OK. I can probably finish off 'the case of the dodgy phone call' this week and you can make a start on this one."

'The case of the dodgy phone call' was the only other case we had on hand and Micah's ability to hack into telephones would have ensured her a job on the 'News of the World' back in the day.

I started a file on Aaron Stevens. For me, a file used to be a lot of papers stuffed into a manila folder. I have adopted Micah's ways and it is now a double-encrypted collection of ones and zeros on a secure server.

Stevens was a model husband and father with no skeletons in his closet no matter how much I delved into his doings. His wife, the prime suspect in any husband's death, had not taken out a massive insurance policy on him and was marginally worse-off with him dead. I did not have much to work on.

It is surprising how much detective work depends on luck. I am an inveterate browser of the local second-hand bookshops. It was in a back room of Badger Books that I came across a very reasonably priced volume entitled "The gangster elite." It was written by an Aaron Stevens. The blurb on the back cover indicated that it was *the* Aaron Stevens.

I bought it and settled down to read it that evening after taking Barker for his daily walk. It dealt with the lives of the Russian gangsters who benefited from the end of Communism. It was written before they became a popular topic in popular culture. It was not a gripping read despite the potential of the subject matter and I was not particularly surprised that it hadn't come to my attention before.

The significant thing about it was the way Stevens had treated his subject. There is always a danger of glamourising gangsters but he seemed to relish the crimes of his subjects and wrote about them in excessive graphic detail. It is not a crime to write a bad book but it did tarnish the shining image I had of his character.

His bank account had been closed. However, it was possible, using a trick Micah had taught me, to access his online purchasing history. Fortunately, he had taken to the new ways of buying in a big way so within an hour I had a lot of information. Unfortunately, it was unexceptional. No massive purchases had been made.

I was sensitised to the name and address so I noticed an advertisement on Google for a caravan. Mrs Stevens was trying to dispose of something she had no further use for.

"I expect you have happy memories of holidays?" was my opening gambit.

"Mr McLairy, I have many happy memories but, as luck would have it, Aaron was the only one to use the caravan. It was parked in the Lyme Regis area. It was quite a remote spot, not an official caravan site with facilities. From everything Aaron said it seemed a bit Spartan so Gary and I never went there."

"How often did Aaron go there?"

"Recently hardly at all but he used to pop down for the odd weekend."

"What is there to do in Lyme?"

"I've never been there so you would have to ask the tourist office."

After that uninformative exchange, I faced the long journey to Lyme Regis. Fortunately, I didn't have to go alone because Micah had filed a report on the "Case of the Dodgy Phonecall" and we shared the driving.

The caravan was quite difficult to find, parked in a remote spot away from human habitation.

"This lock is rusted to Hell."

Micah, as you would expect, had a can of three-in-one in her bag and a combination of lubrication and brute force got us into the caravan. It smelt of damp and I wished Mrs Stephens luck in trying to sell it to any genuine buyers. The accommodation was as basic as possible and everything showed signs of mould. It had been cleaned thoroughly but that was ancient history.

When we had finished going over the repulsive place with a fine tooth comb and finding nothing we decided to find the nearest Inn. Google was equal to the task and we were soon enjoying a passable Merlot in the Dog and Ferret.

The barman was new but "old Barney" was due in later and he had worked at the Dog and Ferret "man and boy since the dawn of time." In the interval, we essayed the Cabernet Sauvignon but it came from a bottle which had been opened around the time old Barney was a boy and it was a mite off. We reverted to the Merlot.

We made sure to buy old Barney a drink and after a bit of chat about the weather we raised the matter of the caravan.

"Ah," was his remark but it was apparent that he was thinking things over slowly.

Eventually, he said, "they haven't been in a month of Sundays but back in the day, that would be ten years or more ago now, time goes so fast don't you find?"

"Yes."

"Well, they used to come here regularly."

"They?"

"That's what I said. Two of them. Three one time."

I produced a photo of Aaron Stephens and after taking his glasses off to look at it, old Barney said he looked a bit like but the photo was of a man older than the one he remembered.

On the off chance, I also produced a photo of Colin Spelman.

Bingo! Old Barney recognised him right away.

"Have you got any more photos there, Mr McLairy? I recollect there was once a third man."

"No, can you describe him?"

"I can do better than that if you wait a moment."

In a back room, there was a pile of newspaper cuttings. As he sorted through them, he talked.

"The two of them came in here for a couple of drinks as normal and they had this friend with them. The thing was he seemed to get really drunk quick. The others said it was because he wasn't used to the drink and they very kindly took him home with them. They practically had to carry him off the premises but they were laughing and joking about it at the time. Ah, here we are,"

He produced a yellowing old newspaper with a photofit of the third man. The story read,

"The corpse of a young man was washed up on the beach. The police have released a photofit which is as close as they can get to a picture of the body given the decomposed nature of the corpse which had been in the sea for a number of weeks."

Old Barney continued, "I told them all about the young chap but they were not likely to believe me. You see, Mr McLairy I was a bit of a tearaway in my youth and had a mess of trouble with the local police. As far as I was concerned I'd said my piece and it was up to them whether they believed me. I got off the premises before they thought of something to arrest me for."

"I'm a law-abiding citizen now. I reckon I'm too old for any larks these days."

We had a few more drinks with old Barney and although he talked enough, there seemed to be no more information to be had. The police had never found out the identity of the young man and the local belief was that he fell off the cliff into the sea and the fall killed him. We were not so sure.

Micah wrote all this up in a long email to Inspector Tillotson that night. She photographed old Barney's newspaper clipping and emailed that too for good measure.

Inspector Tillotson's response to this was remarkable. In a PGP-encrypted email, he let us into rather more information than he should have done.

"The photo closely matches that of a missing person from twelve years back. Mr Karel Pichowski was a Worthing resident. He was kidnapped and his wife, now deceased, received a ransom demand. Against our advice, she paid the ransom, as she later admitted to us when the kidnappers failed to return her husband. There are thousands of missing persons and it is not unknown for erring husbands to fake their own kidnapping. Eventually, the investigation was wound down. The only remaining relative is the daughter, Rhoda Pichowski.

"We know that Rhoda continued to pursue the mystery of her father's kidnapping and we could expect frequent telephone calls from her inquiring into the case. She did not pass on any information to us. Then something strange happened. Her calls ceased. I left it for a month then personally and discreetly checked if she was alive and well. She said she had decided to get on with her life. I couldn't argue with that. I think it best if you convey the information to her. I have a particular reason for asking you to do this."

Having spent the night in what passed for comfort in the Dog and Ferret, we had the long journey home.

"Are you thinking what I'm thinking?"

"I don't theorise in advance of the facts," Micah said. This was very proper and completely untrue.

"I wonder where Rhoda went on holiday," I said.

"So do I," she said, "so do I."

"Rhoda, I think I may have some information about your father."

"I have had reporters, charlatans and clairvoyants say the same thing."

"Did they have photographic evidence?"

There was a pause.

"No of course not."

I handed over an enhanced printout of the newspaper article.

"Do you think that might be your father? It is a photofit."

"I know."

"You've seen it before?"

"Yes."

"In Lyme Regis?"

"I go there every year. I knew it was a place my father used to go and I somehow felt close to him there. That must sound silly."

"It doesn't, Rhoda. And when did you see that picture?"

"It was a rainy day in Lyme. They have a lot of them. I went to the local library. I'd been there before, reading the local news. They had a new microfilm collection of the archives of the local rag. I was browsing through it when I caught sight of the picture. I scrolled back and read the story. Of course, the thing the local police didn't know was that it was no accident. My father was kidnapped and the dates indicate the kidnappers killed him within a day but still collected the ransom."

"And you told the police about this?"

"Police!" the word held a world of contempt.

"You said, 'kidnappers' not kidnapper. Why was that?" I asked.

"Kidnapper, kidnappers. Whatever. I have talked to you long enough Mr McLairy. You haven't any new information for me so I will show you the door."

And she did.

I had noticed a laptop in the living room. It took Micah all of an hour to hack into it remotely. Rhoda knew her stuff with computers but it wasn't long before Micah knew all she knew. The story was a very strange one but after a further hour, Micah had pieced it all together.

"To start with, Rhoda did a lot more than visit the local library. Once she had the story she investigated the coast between Lyme Regis and Seaton and, fortunately for us, she kept meticulous notes about every house, mobile home and caravan in the vicinity. Eventually, she had enough information to confront Colin Spelman. He claimed that it was just a terrible accident. They had drugged her father with Rohypnol – it didn't have its blue dye because it was the generic version. It was in his cider. Rough cider can get someone very drunk as you no doubt remember."

I did.

"They kept him in the caravan. They assumed that he would be unconscious. He was not restrained in any way. They were very amateur kidnappers. In the night he wandered off in the dark and, in Colin Spelman's version of events, he fell to his death."

"She says, 'I let him think that I believed this hogwash.'"

"The rest of her notes are about selectively reprogramming a 'keep fit' watch."

"One of those devices to nag you into taking more exercise?" I asked.

"Yes."

'It was a bit of a coincidence they both had one," I said.

"They didn't. Spelman received one as a free gift through the post on condition that he wrote a report on its performance. She reports how she forced him to more and more ridiculous excesses of exercise until his heart gave out."

I made a noise as if to speak, she forestalled me.

"No Craig. It is hardly a massive coincidence that they both had heart trouble. Thirty percent of men in their age group die from heart disease and they had additional risk factors. Prior to their rebirth as fitness freaks they had both been morbidly obese smokers."

"She detailed her results as if she were conducting an experiment."

"Which is exactly what she was doing," I said.

Micah nodded.

The watch relayed to her the deterioration of Spelman's health. It fed back to him how much better he was. She recorded the exact moment of his death."

"And stealing the wallets and watches?"

"She couldn't risk the watch falling into the wrong hands and taking the wallet was to make it look like theft."

"And how about Stephens?"

"Her second experiment followed the same pattern as the first. Stephens accepted the free gift on the terms it was offered. He took longer to die than Spelman."

"Is any of this admissible evidence?" I asked.

"You know it isn't," said Micah.

"So."

"We are not going to break into Rhoda's flat and steal her laptop," said Micah.

I knew there was more.

"How about mirrors?"

I thought about this for a moment.

"We set up a mirror of her hard drive. The encryption will be a bit too difficult for the police IT boys and girls to break. Then we tell Inspector Tillotson where it is located."

"Switzerland?"

"No, I fancy a week in France."

"At old Ben's expense?"

Micah smiled and nodded.

Ben Tillotson wasn't at all sure about getting the co-operation of the French police. This was just nonsense. Interpol predates the EU by decades. In the end he just gave in. He got all the evidence we had already seen, a metaphorical smoking gun.

The court took into account the fact that the two had kidnapped and probably murdered Rhoda's father and she got a moderate sentence.

However, if someone offers you a fitness watch for free, my advice is that you should run or at least walk away smartly.

The case of the white bluebell

"Clearly it isn't," Micah said.

"It seems odd to call it a bluebell when it's white," I conceded, "but look at the shape."

"So how come this one is white when every other one in the woods is blue?"

We were making our annual pilgrimage to Clapham Woods. We had caught the brief period when it was a sea of blue. For the first time in our lives we had seen the exceptionally rare white English bluebell.

Barker wanted to investigate the albino flower more closely but we dissuaded him.

We were to discover that, although this one was a unique mutation, Spanish white bluebells are not uncommon and you can buy them online. We also saw our next white bluebell in more sinister circumstances.

We were walking Barker on Durrington Rec when Micah's phone gave an exceptionally irritating tone which indicated a news flash. She resisted looking at it for all of five seconds. I think that is a record.

"I thought this was a nice place when we moved in. Now I'm not so sure. Listen to this. The body of a man has been found. It seems Nicolai Nowak was foolish enough to venture out of doors after dark in Durrington and was the victim of a random stabbing by a person or persons unknown. Mr Nowak had no relatives in the United Kingdom and his family in Poland have been informed by the local law enforcement authorities. No other details have been released to the press. The police are appealing for witnesses," she said.

Within twenty four hours, the police had changed the description of the crime from 'random stabbing' to 'racially-motivated attack." I wondered why, but I didn't wonder long.

Micah is an inveterate twitterer. She showed me the relevant tweet without comment. It showed the body of the unfortunate Mr Nowak. From the lighting it seemed to have been taken at night. The picture clearly showed a white bluebell lying on the chest of the deceased. The text was, "White flower. White power."

"Look like the innocent flower but be the serpent under it," said Micah.

"I don't think we need to add Lady MacBeth to our list of suspects just yet," I said.

"It was tweeted from a spoof IPA."

"The only IPA I know comes in bottles."

"It also comes in cans but you know as well as I do that it stands for Internet Protocol Address. This tweet originated from a fake one and it will be the devil's own job to track it down."

"White Power seems to be the name of an organisation. Does that help us?"

"It's the name of a dozen different groups, all of whom are at daggers drawn with each other so it doesn't take us much further forward. I talked to Inspector Ben Tillotson and the police think that it was the work of a lone assassin which will make him (or indeed her) harder to track down."

"And 'White Power'? In the picture Mr Nowak is white."

"The far right have had to branch out into hating a whole new group of people. They had no tradition of hating Poles so they had to invent it from scratch. We have no simple way to work out who the next victim will be. Poles, West Indians, Jews, disabled people, homosexuals or suspected homosexuals. They have a hate list which includes almost everyone."

"Including you and me?" I asked.

"Well I didn't like to say but of course leftish Catholics score on two counts in the hate matrix."

"Isn't it commonplace for the authorities to assume it is a 'lone gunman' like Lee Harvey Oswald?"

"And it is commonplace for us to keep an open mind until we have more facts to go on," said Micah. I had to agree.

"Now there are a thousand 'likes' for this disgusting picture. I have contacted Twitter to have it removed but at the rate they move it could be a month. The 'likes' could all be sock puppets, fake accounts, but they might not be. The police can probably trace the 'likes' more easily than the original and there may be something there. I will keep an eye on the situation."

"And old Ben?"

"Well he didn't ask for our help but I can keep track of the forensic evidence as he gets it. Let's face it, he knows full well I can do this. That is practically permission to help out."

"Nikolai Nowak was stabbed. So far no witnesses have turned up. The probable time of death was one AM. Now that is interesting."

Micah paused, thinking. "In an aside, the pathologist mentioned that it was not a Spanish white bluebell. That can only mean it is an English one."

"And they are very rare indeed."

"I think we should make another trip to Clapham Woods."

There was still a gay profusion of bluebells in the woods but there was one thing missing. We crossed and recrossed the area where we had seen the white bluebell. It was not there and Barker was able to pinpoint the hole where it had been dug up. He wanted to do a bit of digging on his own account. Fortunately, a bit of bribery and corruption with Mini Woofins dog treats persuaded him to let it alone.

"It could mean nothing," I said.

Micah is usually the cautious one but she was having none of this.

"One in ten thousand bulbs will produce British white bluebells. The chances of someone in Durrington having access to a different source are negligible."

For the rest of the day, we acted the part of outraged conservationists asking visitors to the woods if they had seen anyone picking the rare plant. Apparently, people had seen all sorts of funny business in the woods and some had seen idiots picking bluebells but nobody could positively identify who had taken the white one.

We passed the information on to old Ben Tillotson and words like "irrelevant" and "time-wasting" were used.

Undeterred we intended to go back to the woods the following day but something turned up.

Over breakfast, we listened to More Radio. "Another murder victim has been found in the Worthing area. Goring resident, Mr Anatol Kowalski has been identified as the second victim. He was subjected to a horrific acid attack and died from his injuries before he could be taken to hospital."

"The police are appealing for witnesses. There are unspecified 'similarities' between this crime and the killing of Nicolai Nowak."

A search of Twitter showed us the similarities. Both were Polish. Both had been murdered and "White Power" was proudly taking responsibility. Mr Kowalski's body had been dumped with a white rose for company.

"A Yorkist fanatic?" I asked

"That is not helpful, Craig."

We lacked the manpower to stake out the bluebell woods but Micah's letter in the *Worthing Herald* that week did gain us one helpful witness.

"I saw your letter," there was a voice on the telephone.

I said nothing.

"You aren't interested in any bloody bluebell. I know what you're playing at and you won't get away with it, see?"

"Can I take your name, Mr..."

Even white supremacists aren't stupid enough to fall for that old trick. The phone was put down, quite forcefully.

Naturally, I informed Inspector Tillotson immediately. He got back to me very quickly to say the "boffins" (his word) had been unable to trace the caller.

"Still, look on the bright side, if they kill you, Micah will have a good chance of catching them." He laughed to show it was a joke, of sorts.

The next death was spectacular and it was not immediately apparent that it was a murder. Of all places, it took place at a church. During mass, a member of the congregation suddenly started to vomit what another member of the congregation called "a fountain of blood" which couldn't be stopped. Again an ambulance was called. Again the victim was dead on arrival at Worthing Hospital.

He was named locally as Augustyn Szymanski who was a Worthing resident although his parents came from Belarus back in the days when it was called Byelorussia and was under Stalin's loving care. He was a retired mathematics teacher.

In the middle of the night, someone had left what was originally thought to be a floral tribute at the mortuary. It was a white rampion.

"For a psycho killer, our man (or woman) is quite the horticulturalist," I said.

"It is as if they want to taint every beautiful flower with their sick ideology. Murder and sacrilege. Nobody saw the person who left the flower. The devil looks after his own," Micah said.

The pathologist who had replaced Dr Winter was really quite a pleasant and efficient young man. He had some understanding with Inspector Benjamin Tillotson that he should share intelligence with Micah, whom old Ben described as "the brains of McLairy and McLairy".

"I suggested he have a look at the cork," she said proudly.

"And?"

"A hypodermic needle had been used to inject a complex chemical into the communion wine," she held up her hand to stop my next question, "The reason the whole church was not poisoned is more complex still."

"Have you ever used Araldite?"

There is usually method in Micah's madness so I just nodded.

"The epoxy adhesive only works when you mix tube A and tube B together. This poison works the same way."

I nodded again.

"The substance in the wine was the equivalent of tube A. The victim must have ingested the equivalent of tube B beforehand. If you say anything about a sticky end I really will hit you. On their own, the two complex chemicals were not harmful.   Together..."

She didn't have to finish the sentence.

On cue, the picture of the white rampion appeared on Twitter and was duly retweeted 1024 times. The police had by now established that the retweeters were dead ends because they appeared to be sock puppets or bots. Whichever they were they were using spoof IPAs.

"Our psycho killer seems to be a clever blighter," I said.

"They are foolish. The leaving of the white rampion was a stupid and risky act which could so easily have seen them brought to justice. CCTV is everywhere and it is more by luck than judgement that they have evaded it so far.That is to say the police have been unable to find any useful images. The phone call to you was the height of stupidity. Calls to Durrington Detective Agency are recorded for staff training purposes (although we are the staff). When, not if, when, this killer is caught then it will be as good as a fingerprint to identify him."

"You say, 'they'. You think there is an accomplice?"

"I don't know of course. Jane Austen used 'they' as a singular pronoun. I just have a feeling that this crime and horticulture do not sit well together. I think the horticulturalist would be an excellent witness against the accused when the day of reckoning arrives."

I have never known Micah so positive. I tried to share her upbeat attitude but I thought there would be more death before "they" were brought to justice. I was wrong.

I do not possess a pair of handcuffs. Micah for some reason does. I didn't like to ask.

It was three o'clock in the morning and our mysterious visitor was firmly attached to the kitchen chair with them. We were waiting for the police to arrive. The visitor had a bandage on his nose which made it hard to identify his voice. His face had collided with a bedside lamp. It was the only weapon I had to hand. He bled like a stuck pig... all over my duvet. I considered billing Ben Tillotson for the cleaning.

On the table were a screwdriver and a juicy steak on a piece of tinfoil. I wasn't having stains on the kitchen table as well.

"So you were breaking into our house to do some light repairs and brought a snack?" Micah asked.

He didn't speak. After a stream of vile but snuffled invective when he regained consciousness after the bedside lamp incident he had been as silent as a sullen teenager although I guessed his age to be mid-forties.

"Let me help you out," I said quietly. "To be seen carrying a knife or acid is a dangerous type of behaviour, doubly so if you repeat it. A screwdriver is not an offensive weapon under the meaning of the act. The fact you were about to stab me with it in the middle of the night will probably count against you in court."

"The steak was supposed to incapacitate Barker but he is an intelligent dog. He couldn't tell it was poisoned although I expect the police will do so. He just knew something wasn't right and decided he wanted a piece of you instead. I am sorry about your trousers by the way."

Barker was watching our visitor's every move and the visitor did not appreciate the attention.

"You didn't carry a floral tribute with you this time because the police are wary of anyone carrying white flowers around in the middle of the night in these parts."

Micah took over.

"You're not the horticulturalist, not with those hands. I doubt if you've ever wielded a trowel in anger."

At the word "anger" he exploded with rage.

"My Maisie did all the gardening when she was alive and it was you lot that done her in. Jews, Catholics, foreigners. She would have been still alive if it weren't for you and the bloody EU."

The police arrived and took him away. They gave the handcuffs a funny look but made no comment.

Micah gave Barker a handful of dog treats.

"You're the brains of McLairy and McLairy," she told him.

We later found out that Maisie Gardiner had died from cancer and Harry Gardiner, our visitor, blamed the doctors who had failed to keep her alive. When he found out some of them were the foreigners he had hated to start with, the idea festered in his mind and a horrible revenge was planned.

None of Gardiner's victims were connected with Maisie's death, which was from natural causes, "because then it would have been too easy for you lot to catch me," as he later said during his many interviews with the police.

He also revealed that he had dropped the complex chemical into Augustyn Szymanski's pint in the local pub where he always drank before mass. Traditionally, one is not supposed to eat or drink right before mass but the punishment does seem severe.

Ben Tillotson told us all this in The John Selden and he even bought me a drink. The age of miracles is not past.

Also by the author

If you enjoyed this, you will also enjoy the five books in the #mirrorofeternity series.

The Mirror of Eternity

This is the first in the #mirrorofeternity series. It is a collection of short stories.

In the Mirror of Eternity It is dangerous to meddle in the past and perhaps even to observe it.

Jack London's Suicide Note – a fictitious exploration of the controversy surrounding Jack London's untimely death at the age of 40.

The Library – an encounter between two very different characters in cyberspace. These days libraries have computers and you can meet all sorts of people online.

Der Der, Der Der – the first Virginia Monologue story. Be warned, she might be quite amusing on the page but give her a wide berth in real life!

Guilt App – A story about the life of the rich and the chasm which exists between them and the 'people of the abyss.'

Paradox – Another adventure in cyberspace. The original story even had screenshots from a Commodore 64 but these have been sacrificed as the C64 now seems even more dated than I am.

Here be dragons – a story which explores the possibilities of travel in time and space. The 'dragon' in question may come as a surprise.

After Spartacus – Spartacus could be regarded as the first socialist – he thought the liberation of the oppressed was a job they could not leave to someone else. The Cross did become a symbol of Rome, but not in the way the Romans of the time imagined it would.

The SS Dagger – using the Mirror of Eternity to solve a murder in Nazi Germany produces an unexpected ending.

League of St George – a harmless drinking club celebrating the myth of St George hides something far more sinister.

The Stalker - I read the tabloid headlines most mornings. If the economy is going down the pan, they will have a headline about Big Brother. If the prime minister is at the centre of a scandal, EastEnders will be the big issue of the day. And I wonder exactly what the truth is behind their celebrity stories.

Virginia Monologue – the second Victoria Monologue story sees her talking to a friend who does not seem to be responding.

Doctor, it's about your car - The best way to get through to someone who is too busy to talk to you is to tell the switchboard "It's about his car." You will get through – even if they are "on a trip abroad" or "in a vital meeting" :)

Dramatoes - Childish pronunciation is always endearing. This story grew out of the way my son pronounced "dominoes".

Omar - This story is based on a personal experience when my wife and I were in Tunisia. I can tell you in advance that the ending was somewhat different in our case but that is all I will tell you before you read it.

The Inspector called - A story about a school inspector. You will have guessed by now that I was a teacher once upon a time and they drove me up the wall. Bear with me.

Schadenfreude - The borderland between waking and sleeping is a strange and sometimes frightening place. It is just as well it is 'all in the mind' isn't it?

The Hitch-hiker - "Don't take lifts from strangers" is all very well. But don't forget the hitch-hiker is a stranger too.

Stations of the Cross - I never "really" believed my father was dead. It was only later, much later, that I realised he wasn't dead. Not as long as he was remembered.

The Tower of the Moon - A romantic tryst with a twist.

When I think about you - This story has been rejected by magazines as "too shocking". So either read it and prepare to be shocked or give it a miss!

Salt Wars

Salt Wars is a myth of the foundation of the city-state of Salzburg. Salt Wars is a science fiction book. It contains mild sex and violence. It also contains some humour.

Xavier Hollands is an eccentric technologist. That sounds so much better than "mad scientist". Using his father's theoretical work he has found a way to create a hard astral projection. After testing this out with his girlfriend, Tilly, he is dragged into the Salt Wars by Wolf-Dietrich von Raitenau who wants to secure the future of Salzburg and his own future as its Prince-Archbishop.

They travel back in time to the town which will eventually become Salzburg. Xavier's astral projection is so strong that he comes into conflict with the "best man" of the town whom he defeats at the May Fair. He also develops a relationship with Krystyna, the daughter of his employer in the town and betrothed of the erstwhile best man.

Using Xavier's methods, Tilly intervenes to save Xavier and to thwart Wolf-Dietrich. Magus – a medieval Satanist – tries to use Krystyna to seduce Xavier and thus tie him to the town forever. When this plot fails because of Tilly's intervention there is a battle through time and space.

Wolf-Dietrich is hunted down like a literal wolf. Xavier meets his claustrophobic nightmare on a submarine which is then depth-charged and flooded with water. Tilly meets her fate in a school where she cannot control her class or stop them bullying a young boy called Gabriel. When Tilly realises that Gabriel is trying to push her towards suicide, he is unmasked as Magus.

The trio return to the town to fight the first salt war. Wolf-Dietrich brings about a successful conclusion by playing on the superstitious fears of the attackers.

The book also has diary entries from the characters which give an insight into their thinking.

The book ends with a teaser for the next Xavier Holland's story "The Archbishop's Torturer"..

The Miranda Revolution

Can a mother's love help bring down a vicious dictatorship? The dictator is a strong man but Miranda is a strong woman.

In this book, three characters, Wolf-Dietrich, Tilly and Xavier become involved with the battle to overthrow the Dictatorship. It is an adventure story in which the three of them fight evil in their own very different ways.

The Dictatorship described is generic and could apply to a number of countries. The gangsters control the streets and the Dictatorship controls the gangsters.

The Dictator's consort, Miranda, is drawn into the revolution by realising one of the street-girls is her daughter. A religious movement which has been a safety valve of value to the Dictator is transformed by Miranda's visions through the 'mirror of eternity'

The Miranda Revolution is a book of light and shade. Although there is humour, there is also a serious side to it. Shelly encouraged the poor to seek a better world with the phrase, "Ye are many, they are few." The poor know only too well that the rich have the guns and tanks on their side. The book is a work of fiction but it suggests one way those problems could be overcome. It is a message of hope.

The Miranda Revolution is suitable for young adults. It contains sex and violence but none of it is graphic. Most of the sexual references illustrate the plight of the street-girls in the Dictatorship.

Defending the Sangreal

The fourth book in the #mirrorofeternity series explores such varied scenes as the realm of Arthurian legend and the dark hidden world of Satanism in the UK.

"Joseph of Aramathea brought Christianity to these islands. He did not bring it in a bloody cup!" (Sir Gareth).

A little blunt but to the point. *Defending the Sangreal* gives a new take (Xavier's take) on what the sangreal was all about. It may surprise you. It will give Dan Brown a fit!

So if you have ever wondered what the sangreal (or holy grail) really represented; if you have wondered what kind of horses the four riders of the apocalypse rode or whether there really was a top and bottom of the round table, this book will answer your questions. From a certain point of view.

This book will make you want to know more about the knights of the soi-disant 'round table' and about the Mirror of Eternity. It might make you want to avoid Satanism and Satanists like the plague. It will certainly intrigue you.

Space Dog Alfred

Space Dog Alfred is not part of the #mirrorofeternity series and it is aimed at a younger audience. It is the book which has had most success in the difficult business of getting libraries ,which have no money to spare, to buy copies.

The book tells the story of a French Bulldog who ends up going into space with Finbar Cool, a very dodgy street trader and uncle to Tom and Seren, the twins who accompany him. Finn brings his daughter, Abby, along too. Tom is delighted about Abby tagging along, Seren not so much.

On the planet they visit there is a group mind which is shared by Gai - sentient tree-like creatures - the Veck who are humans but have mastered unpowered flight and the people of Ardin who are small but perfectly formed. They worship death.

The group mind is not shared by creatures known as the Gnarl who are warlike and largely live underground.

It is an adventure story in which the powers of all the characters are tested to the maximum. Abby, captured by the slovenly Veck, realises that her selfishness is holding her back. Seren eventually comes to realise that Abby can change for the better. Tom finds out that he really doesn't know everything. Finn realises the futility of war. Alfred's bravery and his powers of perception make him into a hero. Like all French Bulldogs, he has the power to understand what humans (and other creatures) are thinking.

In the end good triumphs over evil. The heroes succeed in averting a war which would have cost thousands of lives. In doing so they also introduce the gnarl to the joy of storytelling. They prove that it is possible to win a battle by surrendering.

Domain of Dreams

In this book, I have returned to the short story format. I have had some success in selling short stories in the United States to *Everyday Fiction* and to *Page and Spine* and in Canada to *Saturday Night Reader.* I even had one published in the Worthing Herald! It has something for everyone – adventure, romance, mystery and humour. I put into my stories the things I like to read myself. I expect all writers do that :)

Although science categorically tells you that you cannot travel in time, in your dreams and reveries you can go to any place and any time. I think that Domain of Dreams takes full advantage of the possibilities of the Mirror of Eternity. Opinions differ as to whether it provides access to a parallel universe or its effects are simply an illusion.

The main characters are Wolf-Dietrich von Raitenau, the Prince-Archbishop of Salzburg. Xavier Hollands, the eccentric technologist, his wife Tilly who shares the programming of the Mirror of Eternity and the narrator who has remained a shadowy figure in the previous four books.

I love the scope and freedom which Science Fiction and Fantasy brings. I also like the discipline of the short story. As Mark Twain said in apologising for writing a long letter to a friend, "I didn't have the time to write a short one."

I started writing when I was ten but I have been able to devote the time to it since I retired 50 years later. I have learnt a lot in the last eight years both about writing and about the market for books. I have had some success in selling my self-published books to libraries and bookshops but it has been an interesting challenge.

My greatest joy is sharing my ideas with my wife, Angela, who is also my editor.

Note – I intended to call the book "Dreamscape" but there are a surprising number of books with that title.

Printed in Poland
by Amazon Fulfillment
Poland Sp. z o.o., Wrocław